I0586805

# The Thinking Machine

## The Synthetic Albatross Series
## Book One

AWP

The Thinking Machine
AdventureWorldsPress.com

First Printing. April 2018

This is a work of fiction. Names, characters, places, and incidences are products of the authors imaginations or are used fictionally and are not construed as real. Any resemblance to actual events, locations, organizations, or persons, living or dead, is entirely coincidental.

Published By
Adventure Worlds Press
Windsor Ontario

Printed in Canada.

ISBN 978-0-9949803-3-5 (paperback)

Cover by Sean Meraw
Author Photo by Khoa Nguyen

# The Thinking Machine

## Ben Van Dongen

# FOR MY BROTHERS

# One
## The Giant

Zed. The name ran through his head as the train slipped underground. Zed. It was his name and it was the name of something else—something wrong. A row of yellowed lights along the ceiling blinked, struggling to illuminate the car. Some of them remained dark, long dead. Zed stood near the back door, leaning against a pole. He listened to the squeaks and screeches of the metal wheels on the metal tracks. He'd gotten used to the speed. When he caught the stop at the farthest edge of the huge city, he'd fought to keep from being sick.

The trip from the first stop took Zed five days. He guessed a local would have managed in fewer, but the frequent switches to other trains on other lines tripped him up. The stations, laid out like a subterranean maze, caused him to miss departures, and one time, go in the wrong direction.

He wasn't sure how the people did it—memorizing the labyrinth, all the tracks and tunnels weaving their way through a city that grew like cheatgrass, overtaking everything around it. He'd heard about cave-ins. Tunnels that collapsed under the weight of the buildings above or just eroded in time. Other riders mentioned recent collapses somewhere in the city that slowed down the ceaseless churn of people.

The train reached a bend and Zed saw sparks illuminate the tunnel with a flash. They slowed and the car shuddered. He swallowed, gritting his teeth until the ride smoothed out again. A woman sitting across from him fell asleep, her pudgy body rolling with the movement of the train. The fifteen other people in the car were awake and active. No matter what time of the day, there seemed to be multitudes of people going about their business. The farther into the city he went, the more people there were. Some wore devices on their ears. All of them stared into nothing in a daze.

His grandmother would have made a sign to ward off evil and call them husks. She would make Zed, her surrogate eyes, search for the escaped ghosts that hid in the border between light and darkness. Zed recognized them as something else. They were like the men he'd seen lost in drink, never whole, always in a stupor.

He searched the edges of the yellowed lights and

watched for movement. He thought about the information he had. The name. A Giant came to him while hunting—the tree sized spirit that children often see. It told him to go into the city to destroy the other Zed. The rest was in his hands. The only information he'd been able to gather was that he had to find a broker. Someone with the ability to find the information he needed.

The brakes engaged, throwing up more flashes in the tunnel. The train jerked as it slowed to a stop. Zed put his face to the window and peered into the darkness. He saw an open space, something beyond where the tunnel walls should have been, but it was too dark to see anything else. In the reflection, he saw the sleeping woman was slumped forward in her seat, snoring.

The rest of the passengers moved to the far side of the car. A kid with big cups over his ears and a tattoo across his face put up his hood and faced the other direction. He looked like he was shivering, but the train was warm, even uncomfortable. Zed tensed.

He leaned closer to the window until his nose touched the filthy glass. Far back, or extremely dim, lights danced through the empty air. They bobbed and swayed glowing brighter, getting closer. A scream cut through the snoring and the woman flinched.

3

A flame sailed in an arc and smashed against the train, lighting the side with a swath of fire. Zed jumped back. More whoops and screams echoed over each other and several more fires crashed against the car. The blaze was difficult to see through, but Zed made out the dozen or so oddly dressed figures lighting bottles on fire.

The train lurched forward again, causing Zed to stumble.

The speakers built into the ceiling crackled. "Attention passengers." The other people in the car stared at the empty space in front of them. "Due to a disturbance on the Oxley Platform we will not be making our scheduled stop. Please keep your voucher for this trip to receive a transfer for a Skyship or Magtram when we reach the next station. The TXRC apologises for any delay this may cause. Have a pleasant trip."

The fire flickered and snapped, grazing the tunnel walls as the train picked up speed. Overhead a stream of foam poured from the ceiling and doused the train, putting out the fire. The passengers shifted back to the positions they had before the attack, keeping as much space between them as possible. The kid with the head-cups leaned against a pole, sniffing and twitching, making angry faces at nothing. It was the behaviour of a young buck about to clash with an established male.

Zed looked back out the window and watched his reflection as the dark wall moved behind it. The circles under his eyes were deep and his tan skin was sallow. His thin lips were pressed together and his eyebrows arched towards each other, giving him a disapproving look. Taking a deep breath, he stifled a cough, catching the scent of something foul in the enclosed car.

In the windows, he caught the eyes of the old lady then the young buck. He continued to scan the scene and fought the urge to clash antlers. The train rocked and he went with the motion, eager to get out of the confined space. The first time the trains went underground, Zed panicked. The caves in the woods were no place for people. Even bears, the few he'd seen, only ventured underground when nature forced them. The earth was the realm of the Giants and the spirits. The ones who invaded his dreams and sent him into the city.

Light glared in the tunnel ahead and the car entered the station. The brakes whined and the train slowed to a stop. The yellow lights beamed like the sun, forcing Zed to squint. He put his foot out to keep from tumbling forward. A crowd of people, a mix like in the car but much larger, surged forward. The young kid dashed for the door, knocking back an older man. He jumped onto the platform and shoved through the throng as they funnelled through the door. Zed pushed against them, trying to exit, like a salmon swimming against the rapids.

Angry faces turned towards him as he swam off the train. The doors closed with people still pushing to get in. An arm stuck out through the seam between the doors and the face of the man who failed to get off the train, pushed back by the young buck, was pressed against the window.

The floors and walls of the station were tiled. Most of them cracked and dirty, the low ceiling bare concrete. Against a wall, he spotted a symbol marked in streaked red paint. In a rough circle was a hand with two X's marked on the palm. Under it was scribbled the word, 'rise'. No one else bothered with it, so Zed moved on. People milled about, some waiting for the next train, some seemingly meandering, senseless. Zed headed for the stairs at the back of the space. The train disappeared into the tunnel and the resulting whoosh of air pulled at his coat. He fell into a line of people ducking into the stairwell and trudging up the steps. They led to another platform with tracks on both sides and a high, cavernous ceiling. Bridges arched over the tracks and led to the opposite platform where crowds waited.

Zed walked along the narrow centre aisle, ignoring the bridges. He headed for the back where another flight of stairs led up. A metal bar in the middle separated the sides. People poured down the left side and a few walked up on the right. Springing up the steps, Zed passed the individuals in front of him, heading for a narrow shaft of light reflecting off the dull walls. He smelled an approximation of fresh air and was nearly at a run when he crested the top steps onto the street.

When he first reached the edge of the city, he hesitated to cross the line where concrete and steel crumbled into dirt and wood. Machines droned, constantly pushing the city farther, tearing down trees and consuming the land. The sight at the top of the stairs was beyond his dreams. The visions the Giants showed him were shadows of the real thing. Buildings rose up standing on each other, intersecting, connected with hundreds of walkways and cables. They loomed like mountains and touched the sky as if the earth folded in on itself.

Zed stood looking up and was shoved from behind by someone coming up the stairs.

"Out of the way, buddy." The man wore a long coat over his clothes and carried a case. He gave Zed an extra sneer before his gaze shifted to look at the nothing everyone else did in the city.

More people came up the steps and Zed moved, huddling against the nearest wall. He knew his destination, but not where that was. The street was wide, big enough for several of the trains to run along it with room to spare. Vehicles zipped down the inner portion, dodging the hundreds of people who wandered across their path. The mass of people seemed solid. They moved and undulated like bees swarming over a freshly opened hive.

Watching the constant crisscrossing flow, Zed let his mind wander. He needed to find the aberration and didn't know where to start. Staring into space, watching the swarm dance, he let the Giants guide him. He bit his lip and hoped they could reach him in the middle of the city. Something told him to keep heading south, so he jumped into the crowd and pushed his way forward. Eventually, he found a stream of people heading in that direction and joined it. The sun dipped behind the wall of mountainous buildings, like a premature sunset, casting the street in shadow and darkness.

Zed shivered and pulled his coat tighter around himself. Lights lining the street blinked on. Brightly coloured signs came to life. They had been there before, but he hadn't noticed them in the light. They buzzed everywhere he looked, advertising businesses, products, and services. They were beautiful and intricate. Some of them danced and fluttered, luring his attention. It was loud, like pounding rain pierced with cracking lightning. He looked down at the person in front of him and blocked out as much as he could. He didn't know where he was going, but he hoped he'd be there soon.

# Two

## Two Bowls

Zed followed the flow of people, fighting his way to another stream when the mood came over him. He'd left the large street behind and wound his way through roads that seemed like tunnels in comparison. Some of the side streets had vendors set up at carts or hanging out of boxy vehicles. The buildings sometimes crossed completely overhead. The smells assaulted him—sometimes good, like food or the rare scent of plant life, often rancid from piles of refuse or filthy people.

A woman slunk out of the shadows of an alleyway and stood at the edge of a glowing orange light. She wore a tight dress that failed to cover her cleavage. Zed wasn't used to the scantily clad women in the city, but the one in front of him was the most exposed he'd seen.

She stepped out in his way. "Hey sweetie. You

look like you could use a friend."

Perfume radiated around her like a physical wall. It smelled artificially sweet and flowery.

Zed winced. "Do you know where I can find an information broker?"

"Sure I do. A good friend of mine in fact. You got money? I can bring you to him." She leaned forward and pushed her breasts out.

"Where?" Zed backed away.

"You some kind of soft-head?" The woman snickered and leaned against the wall. She pulled a small cylinder from between her cleavage and stuck the end in her nose, inhaling.

"This area, this part of the city. Does it have a name?" Zed furrowed his brow.

"Look, you want some company or not? It's five hundred dollars or fifty tokens." Dropping the cylinder to the ground, the woman sniffed and rolled her head back.

Zed walked around her, re-joining the flow.

"Your loss soft-head."

A cart at the side of the street funnelled people around it. The smell of food cleared away the lingering perfume and Zed stopped. The glowing sign that hung on the side of the wheeled counter said *Yin's* and was marked with symbols he couldn't discern. A few people stood next to the cart, eating from bowls. Zed stepped up to the man at the counter and inhaled the fragrant steam billowing from a pot.

The man bowed. "Hello sir. Good evening. You look like you could use a good meal. No better place in Chinorth than *Yin's*." His accent was thick making the words difficult for Zed to understand.

Zed looked at the posted menu, squinting at the characters.

"I am Yin. Would you like to start with tea?"

"You said Chinorth. Is that what this place is called?"

"Yes, yes. You are at the best food cart in Chinorth." Yin reached under the counter and took out a small round bowl. He took a spouted pot off the stove and filled the bowl with a greenish liquid. He handed it to Zed with another bow.

"You will enjoy this tea. Best you can get outside of China. I import it myself." Yin clasped his hands together and nodded at the cup.

Zed held the tiny bowl by the edges and took a sip. He licked his lips and drained the rest of the cup. The heat shocked his mouth, but he smiled. The tea Zed was used to was made from herbs and pine needles, collected and dried by his grandmother. It was tasty, but the drink Yin offered was delicious.

"More?" Yin held out the pot.

Zed nodded and the man refilled it.

"You see how good my tea is, the food is even

better." Yin gestured to the menu and Zed scanned it again.

"I don't know any of this food."

"Would you like me to choose something special for you?"

"Sure."

With a smile, Yin took out a larger bowl and filled it with items from individual containers recessed into the counter. Zed recognized pork, but the vegetables were unfamiliar. His mouth watered.

Zed watched the other patrons eating at the cart. They focused on the food, though a small group chattered among themselves. Everyone used a pair of sticks to shovel the food into their mouths. Zed leaned forward, peering at them. His stomach rumbled. Sipping more tea, he watched Yin add noodles on top of the mixed ingredients and pour a thick broth over it all.

With a flourish of his hand, Yin swirled a dark sauce into the bowl and mixed it all with a pair of sticks like the ones people ate with. He placed the bowl on the counter in front of Zed, put two more sticks across the top, and bowed again.

"Enjoy."

"Thank you." Smiling, Zed sniffed at the food. Steam rolled up and wafted away on the wind. Using the sticks, he dug in, eating his fill. The flavours were strange but he tipped the bowl and slurped out the last bite.

When he finished, he put the bowl back down on the counter.

Yin cleared it away as soon as it was set down and replaced it with a bill. "Was everything as good as I promised?"

Zed nodded and picked up the slip of paper. He glared at the circled number at the bottom of it. He didn't know how much a meal like that should cost, but he didn't have much money. His father had given him what he could, and the first place Zed went in the city was to sell some goods, but handmade items weren't always valuable.

Taking out a fold from inside his coat pocket, Zed pulled out the bills, counting them as he placed them on the counter.

Yin scooped it all up with another bow. "Anything else before you go?"

Zed stuffed the mostly empty fold back in his pocket. He took a deep breath, ignoring the cost. "Do you know where I could find an information broker?"

"That is a tricky question. Some of those people do bad things. Not legal. You're not looking for that sort of thing, are you? I can't help you with that." Yin stood up straight and peered around the busy street. He leaned close to the table. "What are you looking for?"

13

Following the man's eyes, Zed leaned forward too. "I'm looking for Zed."

Yin shuffled back and slipped off the curb. "What did you say?"

"Zed. Have you—"

Waving his hands frantically, Yin rushed back to the counter. "Do not say that name in this place. It is a bad omen that will bring destruction to my establishment."

Zed furrowed his brow. "I've been sent to find him."

Yin shushed him with a finger to his lips. "I will not speak of it."

Looking down, Zed balled up his hands. "The Giants sent me."

Yin gasped and clutched his chest. "You are from outside the city?" Yin grabbed Zed's face and turned it side to side.

Zed pulled away and met Yin's glare. "Yes."

"You must go. He can't hear you without an implant, but he will hear me." Yin grabbed Zed by the coat and pulled him to his feet.

"I have to find him."

"Go, go now." Yin pushed Zed away from the cart. "You are bad luck."

Zed sighed and pursed his lips. He turned and looked for a gap in the stream of people. Realizing the space wouldn't appear, he prepared to force himself into the torrent. Yin slipped next to him, making him flinch.

"You need a real broker. Sixteen-twenty Liberty Street L, apartment ten, one, four. If you're smart, you'll go home, stay away from her." The man shoved Zed into the flow of people and he was carried away.

# THREE
# ELECTRIC WITCH

The apartment was small. Zed felt as claustrophobic as he had in the train tunnels. The smell of jasmine and sour milk made him scowl. A large computer monitor was the most constant light source. Across the street, lights flickered.

An old woman sat cross-legged in front of the screen. The glow from the monitor showed the deep lines on her face and highlighted the scar that formed a canyon across her cheek. "What's your name?" She had a trace of the same accent as Yin, but mixed with something else.

"Zed." He stood off to the side, crooking his neck and slouching to fit under the low ceiling. He noticed the crone flinch when he spoke.

"You're not Zed. I knew Zed." She caught his eyes in the faint reflection of the screen's glass.

"I'm a Zed."

"You shouldn't give yourself a handle that someone else has, especially not that one."

"I didn't."

The room was still and Zed heard a faint hum in the silence. The woman watched him in the glass, chewing on her frown. Her thin eyebrows met as she stared. "And what do you want with me?"

"I'm looking for the other Zed."

The woman spun around on the spot, nostrils flared, eyes sharp. "Strange thing to be looking for. Where did you hear about him?" Her head cocked slightly.

"Do you know where he is?" He forced his voice to stay level.

"Do you?" she snapped.

Zed stared at the woman.

"Strange thing. If he finds out you exist—what's left of him—you'll have more trouble than you can handle. Bold to be talking about him so openly" The woman's face softened. She looked down at something Zed couldn't make out in the dim outline. "A man named Zed searching for him." She looked up, giving him a better view of the lines and marks on her face, some from age, others unnatural. Judging from the room, Zed didn't think she got into information brokerage for the money.

"Coincidence." Zed swallowed.

"Quite. I'm starting to think you don't even

know what you're looking for."

"I was told that you can give me information."

The woman chuckled. "Who told you?"

"Yin."

She shook her head. "That man needs to learn how to keep his mouth shut. What did he tell you?"

"He said you could get me the information I need." Zed shifted to bend his neck to the other side.

"What else did he tell you?" The old woman smiled.

"Not to get involved with you." He blinked and he became aware of trying not to blink. His eyes watered.

"And here you are."

He shifted again and a loud crack emanated from his shoulders. "What do I call you?"

"You can call me Belle."

"Okay, Belle. How much?"

"Not money, but it'll cost." Her lips curled more severely and met the deep lines around her mouth.

"What?"

"There is something I want that he has. Worth more than the hornets nest of trouble you're about to stir-up." Her smile faded. "I suspect you won't be able to get it but it's too big a risk for me otherwise."

"Sounds like you're sending me to chase my tail." The smell was starting to become a physical thing that pushed at Zed.

19

"Without me, you have nothing. No one knows what I know. No one would be willing to risk what I am. Besides, you end up finding Zed, you're dead." Belle waved a hand.

Zed exhaled slowly, then inhaled through his mouth, trying to avoid the smell. He looked at the woman and the apartment where she lived and swallowed. "What happens if I agree?" He cleared his throat. Rubbing his chin, he felt the day's stubble, rough against his worn fingers.

"We make a bind and I get the information you need." A sharp light reflected in the old crone's eyes. She blinked and it was gone.

"A bind?" Zed watched her face carefully, his lips pressed into a line. He was out of his element in the city, but he knew how to trade.

"Contract with a guarantee for both of us." She touched the crag that spider-webbed across her cheek and let out a sharp laugh that turned into a coughing fit.

Zed managed to not flinch at the unexpected reaction of the woman. He stifled a yawn and fought the urge to fidget. His jaw clenched and unclenched with the random blinking of the lights across the street. "And if I don't get what you want?"

"We pretend we never met."

Closing his eyes, Zed let the world wash over him. He sniffed. "How will I know what to look for?"

"If you find him, if you manage to end him, I will tell you what I need. Worry about getting to him before he gets to you."

Zed chewed on his cheek. "Deal."

The old lady gestured for Zed to sit on one of the rugged cushions she used as chairs, and probably her bed. He squatted down and dropped the last few inches. Dust puffed out of the pillow. He crossed his legs, having to use his hands to guide the manoeuvre.

Belle leaned in and examined each side of his face. "You have no implants?"

"No." Zed leaned away from the woman's boney hands.

"I haven't seen a person without implants since I was a little girl. Where are you from, other Zed?" She squinted one eye and turned the other to face him. The image of the monitor reflected off the open eye. The stream of characters running across the screen looked like it was being generated inside of her.

"Not here." Zed tightened his features, squinting at Belle. His legs hurt, but his neck loosened.

"This city is very large."

The response reminded Zed of his grandmother and he smirked.

"If you come from outside of it, you must have been traveling for a long time. You don't seem to have any serious injuries and you managed to find me without implants."

"What's your point?"

The woman grinned, showing a mix of yellow and black teeth. "Just trying to get a sense of you, stranger Zed."

Zed smiled back, mentally chastised himself, and put on a mask of harsh indifference. The warnings of his family ran through his head.

Belle grabbed his face and pulled it close again. "I'm sorry to have to ruin that clean head of yours, but I'm going to have to give you your first implant, young Zed. And it's going to have to be more than just a pact." She traced the curve of his jaw and around the ear. When she found the spot she liked, behind his left ear, she tapped on it, like she was checking the ripeness of a melon.

"If I don't want one?"

Belle laughed again. Her breath was stale. "No choice."

"I could look elsewhere."

"I promise you, you won't find another person in the city willing or able to help you with a creature like the one you're hunting."

Zed nodded. "Okay."

"You eat at *Yin's*?" She held his head still in one hand and reached back with the other one, feeling for the implant she wanted.

"Yes." Zed looked straight ahead. His hands were clenched and his mouth dry.

"Good." Digging around in a plastic box, Belle pulled out a tiny object like a stubby pine needle and loaded it into a handheld device. It looked like a gun without a barrel. The handle was hollow and at the end were tiny blades. Letting go of Zed, she pressed the trigger and the blades spun around each other, opening a small gap for the device to sit. The implant was pushed into place between them. It had a coil of wire around a glass tube, making it hard to see clearly from where she held it.

The mess looked like it was homemade and he hoped it was more sophisticated than it appeared. "It's going to hurt." Zed grimaced, but drove his expression away.

The old woman nodded. "You're going to be unconscious while this wakes up. It's a more complicated process with this model, but I'll be able to eject this one after." She took a deep breath, Zed mimicked her, except she coughed and he inhaled it.

The woman jabbed Zed with the device, sending the implant to find its optimal location. Zed managed to not flinch at the initial pain, but blacked out the moment the implant moved on its own.

# Four

## The Implant

When Zed woke, he realized why the woman had asked when he'd eaten last. His head hurt worse than anything he felt before and every movement made him gag. It was like he was swimming in pain and there was no safe shore. He was scared to open his eyes in case it made things worse. All he could hear was rhythmic pounding that, after minutes of acclimation, cleared into the sound Belle typing. Every keystroke made him cringe. The violence of the keys lessened and the pattern of it almost lulled him back to sleep. He wouldn't have minded passing out again, not feel the thing in his head trying to kill him, but he wanted to find out if there was something the woman could do to ease the pain.

Zed peeled his eyes open and licked his lips. He had to stop halfway through the simple action due to the aggravation it caused. He wanted to clear his throat, but thought better of it. He struggled to breath and let out a squeak.

"Want something for the pain?" Belle kept typing. "Sorry, nothing's going to help but time. I'd pass out again if I were you. The next step is initialization and it isn't going to feel any better. Hang on, I'm connecting now."

Her tone was soothing and Zed was surprised at the sympathy. He knew she must have gone through the process too, but she likely delighted in his struggle with something that was old hat for her. He chalked it up to pride and wavered under a new surge of pain.

The room went white, then flashed through a stream of colour that Zed could feel flood his brain. He reached out to touch anything, trying to connect with the physical location, trying to convince himself what he saw wasn't real. His hand felt the peeled and broken linoleum floor. The force with which he pawed at it caused him to scratch his hand on a sharp corner. The feeling was unpleasant, but visceral, vital. He clung to the throbbing, anchoring his mind to the injured flesh.

The shabby apartment surged into his view as the colours paled and disappeared. Zed could see, and he was happy that he only hurt a lot. He coughed and reached back to feel the cut behind his ear. The area was hot and slick. Pulling his hand away, he expected to see blood but it was a clear gel that the woman must have put there. The spot itched and his fingers flexed at the desire to scratch it.

The room was dark except for the monitor. The shape of the hunched old woman was silhouetted against it. The tapping sound that came from the figure was annoying, but it didn't hurt.

"You're still here." The woman stayed focused on the screen. "You have a new appreciation for the apple after the worm, I bet."

"What?" Zed's hoarse voice sounded funny in his head.

"Something he told me once." She sighed.

Zed could see her eyes shift focus, looking at the something that wasn't there.

"Are you ready to give it a try?" The corner of her lip curled.

"Can it wait until I can think straight?" Zed sat up slowly.

"Not if you want a shot at getting to Zed. Ready?" Not waiting for an answer, fingers flew across the keyboard, starting strings of letters and numbers dancing across the screen.

Zed felt a buzzing in his ear. Flashes of light, like the glowing signs in the city, swirled in his left eye. He blinked to clear them away and heard a high-pitched sound.

"Ah, we have activity."

Zed heard the words both from across the small room and from inside his ear. He flinched and stuck a finger in his ear to clean it out.

"Wonderful. Now to check the visuals." More furious typing preceded a flash in Zed's eye that formed into a video feed of the back of his head.

He closed his right eye and waved his arm, zeroing in on the camera. He turned around but couldn't spot it in the dark. The image changed and he lost interest.

"What do you see now?" the woman asked.

"A map." Zed looked around, adjusting to the image floating above what his left eye saw. He focused on it and it became opaque, when he peered beyond it, the map faded. His mouth hung open and he leaned forward.

The woman chuckled. "Our brains are amazing things. You'll find you'll be able to use the implant more fluidly in no time. It's a special model I tweaked myself."

She sat straighter for a moment, Zed noticed her head held higher too.

"Don't push yourself too hard, too fast. The headache will get much worse if you don't rest." The woman turned back to her screen. "I can monitor your brainwaves and base vitals from here."

"How much can you tell?" Zed tried to see the monitor around her bulk.

"Not to worry young Zed. I can tell much, but my network is the most secure in the city—more than the police or the corporations. You will be safe with me. There is only one thing to fear in the network. The ghost of Zed haunts the city's servers. He has his ways in and out of anywhere he desires to go, but I know how he moves. I can keep him at arms length." She nodded at him then went back to her digital tasks.

"It's fine to make promises, but I don't know you." Zed swallowed and tried to look away from the superimposed image he was forced to see.

"Breathe, new Zed. I can see you struggle without having to look at the data. You are the one who came to me and I am helping you. You have strength, but your strength is not suited for my world." She let the sound of the city, and her technology, fill the space. "You can cut the feed. I'm not so dispassionate." She shifted herself and looked back. Her face was covered in shadow, but her voice reminded Zed of his grandmother.

He closed his eyes and focused on his breathing. He remembered his uncle teaching him to shoot, with patience, focus, and calm. He told himself to turn off the image. He willed the map to fade away.

"Just think about it, don't force it."

Zed opened his eyes, his sight was clear. He had worried there would be a ghost of it still there, but

29

# FIVE

## VENTURE FORTH

Zed heard the snores of the old woman and shut his eyes tighter. Sleeping on the dirty floor was uncomfortable, but it helped with the kink in his neck. Belle had offered him some of her cushions, but he declined. They may have been more comfortable, but they were also filthier than the floor. Rolling onto his side, he saw the woman a few feet away. He sat up and looked around the small apartment. He considered going out, but grimaced at the idea. The room was cramped, but relatively secure. He had already found solace in it.

He stared at the ceiling and traced the watermarks and stains to their origins. A scuttling sound next to him made him sit up. A roach ran for the cover of the shadows. Zed ignored the sensation of crawling on his skin and shuffled to the window behind Belle's large monitor.

There were dirty sheets pinned up as curtains, worn, like the old woman. Light leaked in through the cracks and holes. Zed pulled a sheet back and looked down at the street. Buildings shot up around them, built on top of older, smaller ones, climbing out of view. Zed realized that the light he saw would dip behind one of the monolithic structures soon, blocking out the only sun the street saw that day.

Years ago, on a trip with his grandfather, Zed saw ancient trees in the forest that towered over him, seeming to hold up the sky. They would have been dwarfed in the city. The smallest building he had seen, back at the edge, would have made the tree seem like a sapling.

The memory reminded him of the lessons the old man taught him. Tracking, stealth, patience, hard work. They served him in the city.

Belle shifted and Zed let the sheet close.

"Still here?" Belle coughed, loosening something in her throat.

"Uh huh." Zed went back to where he had slept.

"I had a dream. I thought you were a part of it, but here you are, new Zed." Belle rocked herself back to a sitting position. "Feel like going for a walk?"

Zed nodded. He thought the old woman looked like a corpse in the daylight. Her dark skin was sallow and loose, dangling from her frame. The only weight she seemed to have was in her legs and backside.

"You don't seem very eager."

"Doesn't matter."

"Well, don't worry too much, I just need you to get some eggs for our breakfast. I haven't had a real breakfast in months. I don't get out much myself." Belle coughed more and held her hand up when Zed moved to help her.

She turned on her screen and booted up Zed's implant. He saw her travel to other places through the monitor, reaching out and manipulating the imaginary world. An image appeared in his left eye, he blinked and it came into focus. It showed a dollar symbol with an asterisk next to it.

"Unlimited funds. A little present for helping me out." Belle winked. "They'll catch on eventually and shut it down, but we shouldn't need it by then."

Zed nodded and got to his feet, ducking under the low ceiling. He went to the door and walked out. Shrugging as he walked down the steps, he adjusted his leather jacket, made from a buck his father hunted, and sewn by his mother. He thought of the woman, wondered about her worrying about him— so far from home. He sniffed and felt the material at his sleeve.

A sound buzzed in his ear as he stepped onto the busy street. Belle cleared her throat again.

"The place that sells the eggs is in a building

across the street and twenty-five floors up. On the way you can pick up a gun from a place on the sixth floor. How good a shot are you?"

"I'm good with a rifle." People brushed passed Zed as he stood in the doorway. They turned to the side to get by. He wasn't sure what time it was, but he didn't think it mattered. Hundreds of millions of people lived on top of each other, all sleeping and living on their own schedule, constantly filling the roads, sidewalks, and small alleyways around the giant buildings. Squinting like his grandfather always did, Zed elbowed his way across the street. Small cars and bikes drove everywhere and in every direction, including sidewalks and alleys, and the pedestrians didn't move for them. The flow of people continued in every direction. Vehicles trying to move through them honked, and the signs flashed and danced.

"That's not so good here. You'll get a handgun like everyone else."

"Uh huh." Zed jumped out of the way of a bike.

"Don't sound so glum. You probably won't have to use it. It's more for intimidation than anything."

Zed heard clacking in his head like a more distant sound of Belle typing. A marker appeared in his left eye, indicating the floor and apartment number of his first destination. He nodded to himself, thankful for the information. He didn't want to look like a tourist, especially in the less pleasant part of town where information brokers hid.

Following the marker only visible to him, Zed went through the doorway. Inside the lobby was a set of locked cubbies and an elevator. Zed looked for stairs, but didn't see any. The implant highlighted the button on the wall, and he pushed it. After a short wait, the doors opened with a ding. Inside the small space, the button for the sixth floor blinked at him. He grimaced as he pressed it and the doors closed again.

When the elevator stopped on floor six, the doors glowed and flashed and an arrow appeared, floating in the hallway. He rubbed his left eye and blinked.

"What's wrong?" Belle's voice in his ear made Zed flinch.

"It's a bit distracting."

"Concentrate. Turn off what you don't want to see."

Taking deep breath, Zed willed the arrow to disappear. It vanished. He smiled, but the elevator doors began to close. He jumped out, causing them to halt and retract.

"I don't like those."

"Elevators? Too bad. Anything above a dozen or so floors and you'll be happy they're around."

Zed made his way to the apartment marked by the implant and knocked. He heard shuffling behind the door.

"Who is it?" The deep voice was muffled behind the wood.

"I'm here for a gun."

The door flew open and a big man grabbed him by his coat and pulled him inside. The man was tall and broad, nearly twice the size of Zed. His skin was dark, like Belle's but more rich.

"Don't just shout that in the hallway. Who the hell are you anyway?" The man closed the door.

"I'm Zed—"

The big man jumped back, his eyes wide. "What the hell did you just say?"

"Belle sent me to get a gun." Zed squinted, his mouth tight.

The man looked at him sideways and sneered. "Sure. That old bat has a sick sense of humour. You can call me Tinker."

Tinker walked into another room. "Come on, then."

As Zed followed, he glanced around the apartment. It was twice the size of Belle's. Even the large Tinker didn't have to duck. The adjoining room was a narrow kitchen with a slick surfaced table and cupboards thick with paint.

Tinker was at the far end, pulling out a bag from the top shelf. He walked over to the table and placed the bag on top, gesturing for Zed to sit. "I've got something I think would suit you. You've got a weird vibe, carry yourself bigger than you are."

Zed stared back at the big man, his face placid.

"That's what I'm talking about. This piece is special. Rare, like yourself." Taking out a stubby revolver, Tinker laid it on the table with a thud. "Go on. Try it out."

Zed picked up the dark metal gun. It filled his hand and weighed it down. The barrel was wide, nearly as big as his rifle.

Tinker smiled. "Now, a piece like that makes a man hesitate. It's just your style, but it doesn't come cheap."

Belle spoke up in Zed's ear. "Get on with it. I'm getting hungry and any gun will do."

Zed looked up at Tinker. "How much?"

The man chuckled. "Glad you asked. That jacket of yours, it looks like it could almost be the real thing."

"Not for sale."

Laughing harder, Tinker put up his hands. "Hold on now. We're just talking. I was trying to cut you a deal. I could let this piece go for the jacket, complete with all the ammo you'll need—or it'll cost you a thousand."

"Deal." Zed went to put the gun in his pocket, but Tinker grabbed his wrist.

"Tokens."

"Deal."

Tinker scrunched up his face and his mouth opened. He let go and Zed finished putting the pistol in his pocket. It fit snugly.

Belle chimed in again. "Just look that big mouth in the eyes and think about transferring the money. Should do the trick, and shut him up for once."

Tinker stared at his own floating images that Zed couldn't see. He smiled and looked down.

"Well. There we have it." He pulled out a box of ammo and placed it in front of Zed. "Care to get a lesson on loading that thing? After that much cash I'll even throw it in for free."

Zed stood, scooped up the box, and placed it in his other pocket. "No thanks." He headed for the door.

"Bad man, eh? Watch out for yourself, Bad Man." Tinker stayed in the kitchen, laughing.

Zed took the stairs to the top of the old building. It served as a footing for a newer skyscraper. Girders ran through the roof and around the outside walls to the ground. Thick cables, bigger around than Zed, dangled from the underside of the huge skyscraper and into a junction box. Smaller cables spread out from the box in all directions like an octopus, connecting with other boxes or running straight into buildings. Several were strung across the street, making an unintentional web.

A woman with a plume of red hair stood at a table next to a coop. A rickety shack peeked up from behind the scene. It howled as wind rushed through it. On the side, faded from sun and rain, was the same symbol he'd seen in the underground train station.

Zed stepped over as the woman swung down with a large knife, chopping the head off a bird. "I'm here to buy eggs."

"One minute." The woman tossed the body into a container with others and scraped the head to the side with the knife.

"That an Orpington?" Zed looked at the orange-yellow plucked feathers blowing away in the wind.

The woman stopped and looked at him. She wiped her brow with her sleeve. "You know your poultry?"

"Some." Zed smiled.

"You wanted eggs?" The redhead walked over to a wicker basket by the coop. "How many?"

"A dozen I suppose."

She filled a bag and handed it over, smiling. Zed struggled to transfer the payment.

"Sorry. Thank you for the eggs." When the payment went through, he headed for the stairwell.

The woman waved. "Happy to meet a man who knows something about chickens."

Before he let the door close behind him, he listened to the familiar sounds of the birds.

# Six

## Tallman

Zed went back down to the street. Belle spoke to him through the implant.

"Not bad, little Zed. You hold yourself well, makes the people move out of your way."

"You can tell that from the camera in my head?" Zed looked to see if talking to himself drew any attention, but most people were doing the same or were engrossed with projections of their own.

"And the remote cameras I accessed. You're wiry, but stand straight. It should help."

Zed watched the people clamour by. They fussed about in their own little world like the clucking chickens in their coop, talking to no one. He could hear his grandmother tell him how the spirits of the woods would entrance people who lost their way. A woman walked into Zed and moved on, not commenting or even reacting to the collision.

Holding his head high, Zed walked through the crowd, back to Belle's building. He ascended the stairs feeling confident after his accomplishment.

Belle rubbed her wrinkled hands together, accepting the eggs. She licked her lips as she carried them to the hotplate. "How about scrambled?"

They ate the eggs with more rice and a different sauce as the old woman checked several programs she had running on her server.

"You're going to have to go on another scavenger hunt."

Zed nodded with a mouth full.

"I can find the people you need to talk to, you get the info, and I'll put the map together for you. With luck, and some intimidation, we'll have our hands on the information."

Swallowing, Zed scooped up more eggs on the little sticks. "Then you tell me where to find—"

Belle flinched and her fingers froze on the keys. "You need to watch the names you invoke. You don't want to wake something you're not prepared for. Besides. You stick to your tasks and he'll likely find you."

Zed finished eating. He checked for more, but it was all gone. His stomach rumbled as Belle went back to typing. He followed along as she called up an image of his first target, along with his location, and how to get there.

"This is Tallman." Belle pointed a crooked finger at the picture. "He runs the small-time crime in the neighbourhood. He is connected, but not as dangerous as he wants people to think. He will have security with him though."

The picture was of a young Asian man looking over his shoulder. He wore a red suit with different coloured swirls cascading down the fabric. His hair was spiked, adding to his height. Zed thought of the young man on the train who forced a fierce expression he couldn't back up.

Belle switched to an overhead map of the area. "He has an office in the back of a restaurant a few blocks away." The map zoomed onto the spot. "He spends most of his time there. He'll know who we have to see next. He isn't part of the local syndicate, but he pays up the line."

Zed sat up straight and clenched his jaw.

"Follow your display. Just call it up." Belle smiled.

Zed threw on his jacket. He left the apartment and Belle's voice came over the implant as he descended the stairs.

"You should be fine, but don't push too hard—he has a reputation to keep. Ask him how to find Harmony."

Zed thought the woman sounded more alive in his ear. Creasing his brow he wondered if it was an effect of the implant or the situation. "Should I ask how you know these things?"

"You can."

Zed squinted with effort and brought up the map on the display. It took two tries and made his head swim, but it was easier than he had expected. A marked path hovered in front of him and he followed it.

Words appeared over the places he looked, describing and commenting on his surroundings. *Good Food* popped up next to a small place that looked like it could have been run by roaches and rats. *Do Not Enter, No Access*, was posted in front of an alleyway. Zed avoided it.

Every block had at least a few virtual signs commenting on places or displayed by people. One woman advertised something that made Zed blush.

He followed the marked route and surged through the milling people and tried to stay on task. The sun was already sliding behind one of the huge buildings, cutting off the natural light to the street, the temperature falling. By the time he was on the right block it was an artificial night. He tensed and felt a trickle of sweat run down his back. Neon signs caught his eye and yellow streetlights pushed the shadows together at their edges. Zed kept his expression rigid, but broke the demeanour to jump out of the way of a bucket of sewage tossed out a window.

He recomposed himself, gave a general scowl to the street and found the restaurant where he could find Tallman.

The front of the building had a torn awning that said *ow's* Asia, corrected to Chow's Asian Cuisine in floating letters. The prompt suspended over the sign read *Watch Out*. A menu was stuck on the door. All the writing was in the same symbols as *Yin's* cart, but the implant translated it all for Zed. He noticed that they served rabbit and licked his lips. He decided to try it if he had the time.

The door creaked as he opened it and a chime sounded from somewhere in the back of the room. Two large men stood up from chairs stationed at either side of the door and blocked Zed's path. A woman in an apron scurried over, brandishing a wooden spoon, and yelled at them in a language Zed didn't understand. The implant supplied the English version. It came out garbled though, a note in the corner of Zed's vision said the slang used wasn't in Belle's databanks.

"You two [failure to translate], stop bothering the customers. I still have to run [failure to translate] business."

She rescued Zed from the men and directed him to an open table. He was the only customer other than the two men, dressed in suits like the ones at the door, sitting at a booth in the corner.

47

"Hello fine customer. What do you hungry for?"

Zed thought the translation needed some work, but sat when the woman pulled out a chair for him.

"Rabbit." Zed shrank back when he spoke. He didn't know how she would understand him.

"Good choice, very fresh. I'll bring it right out." She disappeared back into the kitchen and a pretty young girl came out with tea and a sprout filled pastry.

Zed smiled at the tea, remember the tasty brew at *Yin's*. He took a sip and smirked. It was good, but Yin's was better—holding up his claim.

The suits at the door watched Zed closely, but the group in the corner were busy eating and laughing. Zed looked around the restaurant while he waited for his food. It was rundown, like everything he had seen in the neighbourhood, but it seemed like the woman tried to keep it clean. There were stains on the trampled red carpet, but the spots were faded, as if someone attempted to scrub them out. The ornate pillars scattered around the place were cracked and the paintings of snakes with big heads and fins were faint.

"Are you stopping to eat?" Belle said in his head.

"Just getting a feel for the place. It got me past the guards at the door," Zed whispered into his tea.

"Don't get too comfy. You have a job to do."

"Do you want me to bring you some home?"

Zed clenched his teeth. He didn't intend to be mean, but her tone was sharp.

"Tallman." Belle cut the connection and a buzzing at the back of his head stopped. He sighed. It was as if a headache subsided that he didn't realize he had.

The door to the restaurant opened, activating the chime. Zed turned to see a young man dressed in a garish pinstripe suit walk thought the dining room and into the kitchen. The men from the booth got up and followed, their meal half eaten. Zed didn't think the guy looked very tall, but it was the same face from the profile. He took another sip of tea and tried to come up with a plan.

One of the men who followed Tallman stopped and stood in the kitchen doorway and Zed could see past him. Tallman spoke to the woman who greeted him. Zed focused, but couldn't get the implant to pick up what they said. Either he didn't have enough control, or it wasn't possible.

The woman held a plate of slop that Zed figured was his food. He sniffed and decided to move. He was halfway to the kitchen before he knew what he was going to do. When he got there, the guard at the door put up his hand to stop him.

The man's face was scrunched and his mouth fell open.

"Hey that my grub?" Zed stuck his head in the

door and pointed at the woman.

Tallman shook his head, exasperated. "We are in the middle of something, go sit down." He kept his eyes on the woman not bothering to look at the offending customer.

"I'm awfully hungry." Zed pushed past the hand at his chest. In one motion he spun the first guard around, took the plate, pushed it into the face of the second, pulled his revolver and had Tallman in a grip from behind, the barrel of the gun against his chin.

"Everybody freeze." Zed scanned the room. He smirked, amazed at how calm he felt.

The second guard wiped rabbit stew from his eyes, but no one else moved. The man at the door hadn't closed his mouth.

"Who the fuck are you?" Tallman struggled, but Zed had a good grip. The not-so-tall man spat on the floor.

"I need some information, then I'm gone."

"You are dead." Tallman looked from guard to guard.

"Not yet." Zed pushed the gun harder into Tallman's chin, forcing a sound. "Tell them to go have a seat."

Tallman hesitated, but the click of the old gun's hammer made him nod at the men.

"Is there a back way out?"

Tallman gestured to the back of the kitchen. Zed

tightened his grip at the action and pulled the man back, keeping the door to the dining room in view. He dragged Tallman through the kitchen and out the back.

The alley was dark and dingy. The grime that fell to the streets collected in the spaces between buildings. A new structure straddled the restaurant and the building next to it, making the alley a dark cave. Garbage and crates from the kitchen were piled by the door.

Zed saw the entrance to the street and turned towards it. His hand twitched around the gun at the sight of freedom. Blending into the constant mass of people would be easily, but he put his back to the wall. He angled his position so he could see if the guards followed or tried to sneak around the front.

"This is really easy." Zed shook his captive. "Where can I find Harmony?"

Tallman chuckled. "Follow the Buddha."

Zed pushed the gun into the man's face.

"They're going to kill you." He looked back at Zed. "You can't get out of this."

"Maybe, but you'll go down with me." Zed waited for Tallman to crack. He focused on his breathing as the sound of the street echoed around the enclosed alley.

"I don't know where that slut is." Tallman's head dropped to his chest.

"Not good enough."

"She used to work for the syndicate, but that was years ago."

Zed felt the hum in his head. He figured Belle was listening in, or maybe recording the conversation. He loosened his hold on Tallman.

"I don't even know if she's still alive."

"Give me something and I'll go."

Tallman's shoulders sank. "She used to live by the docks—that was five, six years ago."

Zed felt the tension leave the man. He wasn't sure if he had actually broken him, or it was a ploy. Maybe Tallman was used to being the whipping boy to his bosses.

"That's good," Belle said in his head.

"Thanks." Zed pushed, sending the Tallman forward a few steps. He held his revolver out and noticed a man peek around the mouth of the alley out of the corner of his eye.

Tallman shuffled away. "You're dead now!"

Zed shot Tallman in the leg. The sound bounced off the narrow walls and was cut off by screaming.

"Sorry. I needed a distraction." Zed backed up. He watched the street and the door. "You'll be fine."

Tallman fell to the ground and held his leg. Blood leaked through his fingers. He hissed and moaned.

"Your boss is injured. You'd better tend to him."

Zed saw the head sneak another look. He held the revolver out to show the bodyguard he was still dangerous.

"We can stand here and let him bleed to death, or you can come out with your pockets empty and I'll be on my way."

Zed jumped out of the way of a gunshot and landed in a pile of cardboard. The guards used the distraction to come around the corner and out the back door. Zed shot the first one in the doorway, slowing down the ones behind.

"Any way out?" Zed sat up among the debris.

"Just the street." Belle sighed and clicked her tongue.

Zed aimed for the guard running down the alley towards him. "Stop there!"

The man raised his gun, but Zed fired first. The bullet caught him in the stomach and he fell, grasping the wound. His gun dropped to his side, forgotten. His face turned pale and vacant.

Zed rolled out of the pile of cardboard and got to his feet. The men in the kitchen were pulling the dead guard in from the doorway. Zed shot at them to keep them inside and ran to the street. Another guard came around the mouth of the alley and Zed fired blindly at him. The noise startled some of the mass of people passing by and Zed pushed through them, keeping his head down. It was difficult to make his way through the dense crowd, but he was quickly swallowed up—indistinguishable. Any pursuit by Tallman's guards would be pointless.

# Seven
# The Docks

Zed followed the prompts that floated in front of him until he found a place that said *Quiet*. The business was a small grocery store that had a wild mix of smells that took Zed out of the moment. It was sandwiched between a gambling den with windows spray-painted black, and a pawnshop with a steel cage enclosing the door. He stood outside of the storefront and sniffed left and right, pinpointing delicious and disgusting smells. A young woman shuffled past him through the door and Zed followed.

The store was dim and chaotic inside. Zed nodded to an old man behind the counter. The man wiped his hands on his stained apron as he watched Zed disappear behind the shelves. Aisles of packages, jars, bags and bottles ran up and down the store. He headed to the back corner, stopping to shake, sniff, or poke at things that caught his attention. The woman from the front door stared at Zed from around a corner.

Zed found an empty aisle and felt into his pocket and pulled out a few bullets from the box Tinker gave him. He loaded them into the empty chambers and tucked the gun away quickly.

"Where to now?" Zed spoke to a jar of yellow mush. He picked it up, pretending to read the ingredients.

"Are you shopping?"

Belle sounded like his first teacher, a harsh cold woman with high expectations and no patience.

"Breaking the trail and assessing my state of readiness. Why, do you need me to pick something up for you?"

"You need to take this seriously. Your cavalier attitude and impudence is going to get you in trouble."

"What's my next job?" Zed spoke louder than he had intended and put the jar down hard. He looked up and down the aisle to see if anyone noticed his outburst.

"Tallman will do the next part for us. He'll have to report the incident up the chain if he wants to stay on their good side. Whoever knows where Harmony is hiding will show us the way."

"So what do I do?" Zed felt his stomach rumble, surrounded by the exotic food, and some things he assumed were food. He licked his lips, remembering he didn't get a chance to taste the rabbit stew.

"I'm keeping tabs on Tallman and his superiors. Head for the docks and ask around. May move things along."

Zed nodded, then felt silly since there was no one there with him. Furrowing his brow, he thought she probably could see him and spotted a camera hanging in the corner. He picked up a few pieces of strange fruit and a jar of pickled beans. The unlimited credit worked with the old man at the counter.

"You'll like that." The translated words floated in front of the man's dirty apron as he put the jar in a bag with the fruit. "Very spicy."

Zed thanked him and walked back into the artificial night. He sighed at the constant din and looked up the street. The giant building that blocked the sun glowed around the edges like the Giants in the moonlight. Standing under the grocery store's awning, he brought up a map to the docks. The arrow that appeared flitted back and forth. Zed blinked and rubbed his eyes, making it go away. He took a breath and tried again. The new arrow was more translucent than before, but it held a single direction, towards the towering skyscraper. He looked up as a rumbling sound punched through the general roar of the street. A train, more sleek than the one that took him underground, tore through the space between two of the more modern buildings. It hung from a track and pulled a funnel of air behind it, stirring up the refuse that gathered in dark corners.

"You'll have to take the Magtram if you want to get to the waterfront today. There is a station on the next block," Belle said.

Zed followed the direction of the tracks around the next corner. A platform hung off the side of the building with people packed onto it. "How do I get there?"

"There should be a stairway in the building. Look for the sign."

Zed spotted 'Magtram' written over a set of double doors and went through them. Inside, there was just the staircase that went up. The line to get on the tram started on the steps, making the space cramped and hot. The line grew longer as Zed waited, and when the train arrived people shoved forward against the flow trying to get off, just like in the underground train, but with less space on the stairs. He managed to get on the tram before the door closed, and it surged forward making his head spin. The city passed by in a blur. He kept his gaze inside the car to keep from being sick and was whisked off to the waterfront.

He got off the tram as close to the docks as he could, but still had to walk the rest of the way. The sun moved past the walls of skyscrapers. Glaring rays reflected off the smooth glass surfaces and eventually reached the street as a dull glow.

Zed stared at the cascading light and thought he saw the dim outline of one of the ethereal Giants look down on him from the city's heights. It seemed to reach a large hand around a slim, jutting spire as it stepped over a thick mass of cables zigzagging over a thoroughfare. Rubbing his eyes, the vision dissipated. He checked the arrow again and headed for the docks.

Free from the towering buildings, the docks were brightly lit by the timid sun. The massive ships the size of city blocks cast blanketing shadows of their own, but they were tiny compared to the skyscrapers. Light splashed between and beyond them, falling dead on the murky water.

It took Zed most of the afternoon to reach his destination. The docks were nestled in a low point, making the area a basin where the filth of the surrounding area drained. From the edge, Zed could see over the field of containers, stacked and sprawling like a labyrinth. Beyond the maze, the entire port was clogged with ships, blocking out most of the view of the water. The nonstop bustle of the streets gave way to the open yard but thousands of workers swarmed around the hundreds of freighters. Zed watched the furious coalescence of cargo being hauled on and off the ships with soaring cranes, and people working with and around the equipment.

Making his way past the forest of containers, Zed reached the waterfront before the sun set. Within the maze he spotted several red splotches that looked like they could have been the symbol at some point, but the wet air must have worn them away.

The water was filthy and smelled foul. The warehouses that lined the harbour had seen years of heavy use with little repair. Zed found a slab of concrete near one of the rundown buildings, close to the action, and sat. He took out his lunch and ate one of the fruits as he watched the ships and workers dance.

The fruit was dull and waxy. The taste was interesting, like a pear and a peach mixed together, but there wasn't much of it. The beans were as spicy as the clerk had warned, but Zed liked them—they had flavour. He ate half the jar, threw his trash into a large pile at the side of the building and walked over to a group of workers taking a break. A cloud of smoke hung around the group and Zed had to fight a cough as he approached.

"Hello." Zed waved at the cloud of smoke. "Anyone know if there are people who live around here?"

A barrel-chested, man in a dirty sweater turned his head. "Piss off."

He spat and Zed had to step back out of the way. The group laughed.

"I'm looking for someone named Harmony."

"I said piss off." The man turned and his cronies fell in behind him.

Zed put up his hands and left. "No problem." He met the same resistance with every group he approached. He fell into the habit of searching for security cameras hanging from light posts or off the sides of the rusted buildings. They felt like eyes and he knew Belle was watching him. He hunched forward as if someone were peering over his shoulder. Shaking away the feeling, he approached a few more groups and asked about Harmony.

Zed spotted a man leaning against the open door of a warehouse, packing a pipe. He went over and offered a light.

"Ah, thank you young man." He stuck his small satchel of tobacco into a coat pocket.

"Welcome." Zed tucked his lighter away. "It's nice to smell some good tobacco. Most people smoke those cigarettes out of the pack."

The man laughed. "Nasty little things. I wish I could ban them from my ship altogether."

"Which one is yours?" Zed looked towards the collection of big vessels jockeying to get into position to load or unload their cargo.

Pointing with his pipe, the man nodded. "Right before us there. The Righteous Dude. Coming in from The West Europe Flats, hauling meat, mostly."

"Must be a long way away."

"Traveling is a lonely life, but the sea has a majesty that calls to some." The man took a long puff and watched crates being carried off his ship. "You don't seem like a seagoing fellow." He chewed his pipe. "Not one for this port either."

"I'm not. I'm looking for someone." Zed sniffed at the smoke. It was different from what he was used to, but it reminded him of his father.

"How rude of me." The man patted down his coat. He pulled a hand rolled cigarette from an inside pocket and handed it to Zed.

"I couldn't." Zed put up a hand.

"I insist, young man. Outsiders must stick together." The man gave his beard a stroke.

Zed took the cigarette and smelled it. It was made from the same tobacco the captain was smoking. "Thank you." He lit it and inhaled. It tasted like a foreign fragrant spice. Zed smiled and took another drag.

The man smiled. "It's a wonderful thing to bring joy to another. What's your name young man?"

"I'm Zed." Putting down his bag, Zed held out his hand.

"You can call me The Captain." The Captain laughed and shook Zed's hand. "Pleasure to meet another wanderer."

Zed laughed and picked up his bag. He felt the weight of the jar inside. "Would you like some pickled beans?" He held the bag out to The Captain.

"What an odd question." The Captain twirled his thick moustache. "As a matter of fact. I would love some." He took the bag and peeked inside.

Taking another puff, Zed let the ash drop off the end of the cigarette. "Do you know a woman named Harmony?"

The Captain smiled. "Another strange question. And again, I just so happen to have knowledge of such a person. A woman who I saw on my last berth—" The Captain chewed on the end of his pipe in thought. "It was five years ago and I'm afraid I don't recall where it was I met with the woman. It was a building under a raised street. That's all I can remember."

"Thank you. I should get going." Zed held up the cigarette, already half gone.

"Good luck young man. I hope you find your Harmony."

The docks were a huge area, almost a city of its own, and Zed had only covered a fraction of the waterfront when Belle contacted him.

"How many times did you get punched?" She choked on a laugh and coughed in his head.

"Any word on Harmony? I didn't get anything worthwhile here." Zed pursed his lips.

"I think the one we want is making his move."

"I'm going to follow him." Zed started to head back to the skyline.

"No need, I'm tracking him."

"What am I supposed to do—keep asking around?"

"No point in that."

Zed stopped and leaned up against a pile of cargo containers. He took off one of his boots and rubbed his foot. "And the time I spent out here doing that?"

Belle didn't answer but Zed could hear her wheezing.

"What am I supposed to do?"

"You figure it out." Belle cut the connection.

Zed felt light headed after the conversation. He watched the sun sink into the acrid water, the last rays of the day reaching through the massive ships. His rumbling stomach urged him to find another meal. He continued back into the city, watching the prompts for a place to eat.

# EIGHT

# HARMONY

The sun played hide-and-seek behind the buildings as Zed walked down the busy streets. Wherever he was, it wasn't as hectic as Chinorth. The constant drone of people and vehicles still permeated everything, but the streets were wider, and cleaner. The cables he got used to seeing dangling from every building were bundled neatly and lashed to walls. They only crossed the street where the Magtram track ran, leaving an open view between the cliff-like walls of the building lined street. Most of the men wore suits and the women were in brightly coloured outfits, their noses in the air. They all gave him a wide berth, which made his trek easier.

Zed stopped in a doorway and flexed his blistered feet. The sea of pavement wreaked havoc on his boots. He was used to weeks of walking in the wilderness, but the city took its toll. Even the mountain pass he'd taken with his cousins to trade with a neighbouring settlement was less exhausting. He spotted a sign across the street that said 'Food' to his implant. The restaurant had metal mesh over its front window. Bright neon signs repeated the claim of quality food and service.

Zed could see a few people in the place and went inside. A 'Please Wait' sign was posted by the door, but a waitress told him to find a seat. He went to the back of the room and slipped into a booth. Getting off his feet felt good, and when the waitress came by with a glass of water, Zed drained it. "The special's a chicken dinner, it's real chicken!" the woman said, refilling Zed's glass.

Zed nodded and finished the refill.

"Alright." She stood next to the table, holding the pitcher of water. "And how are you going to pay for that?"

She tapped a foot, but Zed didn't think she realised it.

"Credit."

The waitress took a hand-held scanner out of her apron and Zed thought the payment to her. The scanner dinged when the transaction went though and the waitress simpered.

"I'm sorry. We have to check."

She filled the glass again, spilling a little. "I'll get that order in right away."

Zed nodded and took another sip of water. He put the glass back down. With his thirst quenched, the taste became overwhelming. He found all the water in the city had a strange, strong flavour. Wrinkling his nose, he pushed it away.

The food came quickly and Zed ate it without taking a break. He knew he was hungry, but hadn't realised how much until he was eating. The fruit and beans didn't do much. He tried to get the implant to tell him how far he'd walked, but he gave up and finished his meal. Pie and coffee followed the dinner.

The pie was awful, made with more tasteless fruit and too much sugar. He was used to the pie his grandmother made with berries his young cousins would pick. The coffee was amazing though. He'd never had coffee before and the first few sips were shockingly bitter, but by the end of the cup he wanted more. The waitress told him to be careful or he'd be up all night. Zed was even more shocked when he found out that coffee had a drug that would make him feel awake. He thought about ordering a fourth cup, but Belle logged onto his implant.

He felt the dinner lurch in his stomach as the message came through.

"Our guy is with Harmony. Get over there. Harmony should know something about where to find him."

Before Zed could ask, a map appeared in his

field of vision. He blinked and rubbed his left eye. Out of all the directions he could have chosen when he left the docks, he luckily hadn't picked the worst one. He was several blocks away from where Harmony was—a good walk on his sore feet.

He thanked the waitress and left, pushing back into the crowds. The sun was gone and real night hit the street. It was different from the temporary blackness that happened through the day. It was colder and the taller buildings were brightly lit, casting shadows to the lower levels.

A light rain had started while he was in the restaurant. The water smelled, giving him a clue as to the foul taste in city. Zed rubbed his fingers together and felt an oily, sticky residue deposited by the raindrops. Some of the smartly dressed people headed for cover, pushing together under eaves and overhangs. The ladies in their bright clothing scurried like multi-coloured squirrels but most were unconcerned and continued on their way, so Zed didn't worry.

He followed the implant's prompts and worked his way down the streets, quickly becoming slick. Bright signs clashed and competed for attention and made rainbow patterns in the oily water. Zed ignored them and willed his implant to block the messages being yelled at him. He was eager to get on with his task and finish with Belle.

Zed turned off the main road, down a side street that lead to a dead end under an overpass beneath the footing of a huge skyscraper. The crowd of people thinned out as he headed farther down the dark street and by the time he reached the end, he was alone. The moment of peace washed over him like the slick rain. Zed stopped and enjoyed the relative solitude. Back at the intersection the city continued to churn and burble, but the sound was as dim as the neon lights that reflected off the gathering puddles. The building at the end of the virtual path was low and long. The exterior was dingy, but bits of red stood out where the brick was chipped. It was as rundown as any of the lower level buildings Zed had seen, but the sign projected by his implant noted Harmony was there. He assumed she would be in a nicer place if she were connected to powerful criminals, but apparently the social divides were stronger than he'd thought. The structure stood alone under one of the massive skyscrapers whose footing came down on a building a block away. A long, tall wall ran to the end of the street and around the back of a lot.

The building looked like an old factory that had become something else and eventually was inhabited by people. A car was parked out front and two men in drab suits stood on either side of the door. They stood tall and alert, comfortable with trouble, so Zed hopped the wall, skirting around them, and went to the back lot.

The rear of the building was solid brick with a handle-less metal door ten feet above the ground. Five feet farther up was a row of small windows. The rise symbol stood out on the door, not faded like the others he'd seen. Ignoring it, he kept looking for a way in.

Zed figured that if he could drop down from the building above Harmony's, he could climb into one of the windows, but he had no idea how he could get to the next level, let alone to the specific building. He didn't even know if he could find a way to get out at the bottom of the huge structure.

Searching around the courtyard, he found a pile of old wood, some broken bottles, and a long dead animal. He tried to pile up the wood, but it was unstable and didn't get him nearly high enough to reach the door. He took a running start and jumped. He hit the wall harder than he had planned, not getting anywhere near the height he needed.

Zed gave up on the back door and sneaked toward the front. He peaked around the corner and saw one of the guards stretch. He walked towards them without a plan—hoping for the best.

The closest guard noticed Zed and yelled at him to stop.

"You can't tell me I can't get into my own house." Zed kept his pace.

The man put out his arm but he made the same mistake as the guards at the Chinese restaurant and let Zed get too close.

Zed grabbed the outstretched arm and pulled, planting the top of his head into the big man's face. The other guard went for his gun, but Zed had already had his drawn and jammed the barrel in the guy's cheek.

Zed squished the guard's nose as the other one held his bloody face. "Don't."

The guard put his hands up, but the bloody one went for his gun. Zed swung his revolver at him, sending him to the ground. The gun was back covering the second guard before he could lower his hands.

"Take your friend and walk away."

"He ain't my friend."

"Take him and go." Zed waved his gun.

The guard picked up his unconscious partner and carried him away from the doors. Zed assumed he would just go around the corner and call for help, or come back running. He hoped he could defuse the situation before that happened.

He pushed open the front door and climbed the stairs inside. From the exterior, he figured several people lived in the building, but the door at the top of the steps opened into one big room separated by partitions. He saw a woman comforting an old man in a shiny suit. They sat at a knotted wooden table with a full tea service. The man's head was in his hands.

Harmony met Zed's gaze as he walked down the inner stairs and over to the table. He pulled out a chair and sat. A cup of tea was ready for him.

"Thanks." He put the bloody gun on the table and picked up the cup.

The man opposite Zed flinched and stared at him. His eyes were red and streaks ran down his cheeks. Teardrops still hung from his jowls.

"Were those your guards?" Zed sipped at the hot tea.

The old man nodded, his hands still out in front of his face.

"I'm sorry, I had to hurt one of them. I'd appreciate it if you'd tell them to stay away from the place for now. I just want to talk."

The man looked from Zed to the bloody gun and then Harmony. She patted his arm and nodded, smiling. The man blinked several times and told whoever was on the other end of his implant to call off his protection. He had to repeat the order, adding vigour to his words and changing his mood. He looked back to Zed and seemed confident despite being caught crying.

"You may as well speak. You won't get out of here alive."

Zed was surprised to hear an accent, one he'd never heard before. "I was hoping you'd be more original. I'm here to talk to her." He indicated Harmony with a motion of his head. He ignored the look the criminal gave him.

"You're Harmony?"

"Yes." She looked directly into Zed's eyes. She scanned them.

"I'm looking for Zed."

Harmony smiled wide, cracking the soothing aura she projected. The whole feeling of the room changed.

"Belle, you there?" She laughed.

Zed figured she had her own connection to the old woman. He topped up his tea and refilled the other cups.

"I'm surprised you found me," Harmony said.

Zed tried to guess at the other half of the conversation without looking like he cared.

"Yeah, he's bold." Harmony looked at Zed. "Where'd you find him?"

Zed and the old man caught each other's roaming looks and Zed shrugged. The criminal boss mimicked the action.

"I suppose that depends on if he can get out of here. You too Belle." Harmony finished the conversation and rejoined the table. "So your name is Zed?" She pursed her lips and squinted at him. "That guy's a ghost now, you know. Belle's worked up about it, but I don't believe in ghosts."

"I do." Zed pulled his hands away.

Harmony smiled and seemed like she was going to laugh again, but stopped and stared him in the face.

"There are no such things, kid." Harmony collected the tea set and took it over to a counter.

"I've seen them. In the woods. When the night is calm, sometimes they're out on the lakes. In the winter, when people are huddled in their homes, they peek in the windows. It's hard to see them when the snow's blowing, but they're there.

Harmony turned and leaned back on the counter. She frowned, still staring.

"My grandmother used to scold me for opening the windows at night. She said they'd get in. I felt sorry for them. She used to say ghosts stuck around because they missed something about people. I don't think they know they're dead yet, so they stick close to the living. How long do you think it would take before someone knew they were dead in a place like this?"

The old man's mouth fell open. He looked at Harmony like a child looking to his mother. Zed figured it was what Harmony was to people. He hadn't intended to say as much as he did, but it felt right. Like the old man crying. Letting something go.

"You're a bit slow aren't you?" Harmony walked back to the table and sat.

Zed blushed, but held his expression. His lips were tight and he could feel pressure behind his eyes. "Where can I find Zed?"

"How would I know? You could check the docks. Maybe you can find The Captain, if he's even there." Harmony flipped her wrist dismissively. "Belle can check for you."

Harmony waved her hand at Zed and the *Righteous Dude* appeared in front of him. It was still being unloaded at crane 318. With a little push the map appeared.

"I was there. I spoke to him. He told me about you."

"That's a fun coincidence." Harmony caressed the words and punctuated them with a trill of laughter that sounded like singing.

"This was a waste of my time." Zed stood.

Harmony frowned. "I could say the same. You're not even as interesting as the first Zed. That little story you babbled about was pathetic."

"Do you have anything else you can tell me?"

Harmony huffed. "I could teach you a few things about manners. The only reason you're still here is because I owe that old bitch."

"Get me out of here then. Give me a clue to finding the other Zed so I can be on my way."

"I told you. The Captain may know someth—"

"And I told you, I spoke with him. So give me something else." Zed clenched his teeth.

Rolling her eyes, Harmony stood. She walked towards a wall, stopped part way, and turned back. "You're a pest."

Zed didn't reply.

"Fine. If it'll get rid of you. It's suicide anyway." Harmony waved her hand dismissively. "You could try the park. It's huge and filled with people who could hardly be called people any more. Though, you may actually fit in." She cocked an eyebrow and smiled. "You'll have to pass the Wall, though."

The man made a shocked sound, like a gasp. "Kowloon."

Zed turned to the old man. "Huh?"

"A walled city. Not the original, but much larger. Dangerous. Lawless."

"I thought this whole place was like that."

Harmony laughed with a snort. "You are so dense. Look. The only other suggestion I have is the park and the park is on the other side of the Wall. If you're stupid enough to cross it, you may find a way to get some information about Zed." She crossed her arms. "If you're so eager to end it all. If you've managed to get on his radar, he's going to find you sooner or later."

Zed nodded and made eye contact with the old man. "I'd like to get out of here. What are the chances you'll let me walk?"

The man blinked and tilted his head to the side.

He looked to Harmony, who smirked at them both, then back to Zed, his mouth still open. He nodded and Zed clapped him on the shoulder.

"Thanks." He put the revolver back in his pocket and walked to the door. "And thanks for the tea."

# Nine
## Discord

Pushing open the outer door, he stuffed his hands in his pockets against the chilly night air. The rain came down harder, splashing against the lot. Several cars were haphazardly parked out front, matching pairs of men stood at each one.

Zed expected the old criminal to keep his word and walked through the group, making sure to keep his pace slow and his head high. When he got to the street, he let himself shudder, doubled over and threw up.

"You're crashing." Belle spoke in his head again.

"Yeah." Zed shivered.

"Don't fall apart. And keep your stupid stories to yourself. You embarrassed me."

Zed didn't answer. He straightened up, wiped his mouth, and headed towards the lights and sounds at the end of the block. Stopping at the outer reaches of the neon rainbow reflected off the wet street, he sneered and imagined putting up a wall between himself and Belle. The thought of the woman in his head made his stomach churn and threatened to make him sick again. Harmony, the woman who on the outside seemed motherly, caring, was nasty and callous. Belle was more concerned with how the vile woman viewed her than Zed or his job.

A steady flow of dirty water ran off a nearby overhang and splashed at his feet. He ducked under the ratty fabric awning and hunched his shoulders. The whole task set out to him seemed like a big joke in the late evening rain. He was deep in the middle of the city bigger than the forest he left, and he had no idea where to go. Shivering, he thought of the people he'd met and the one person he had on his side—a woman who piggy backed in his head, chastising him, using him for her own goals. He wiped his nose and considered his next move, desperately trying to block out Belle.

"What do you think you're doing? Get moving before those guys change their mind and come looking for you." The voice of Belle was muddled in his head, like she was speaking from another room.

"I'm deciding where to go."

"Back to the docks. You heard Harmony. Find The Captain and ask him about Zed."

Zed sniffled. "I already spoke to him. He told

me about Harmony."

"So go ask him about Zed."

"That's a waste of my time. Harmony told me about the park."

"The Park is a wild zone. Anyone in there is an animal now. Besides, to get there from where you are, you'd have to cross the Wall. Even I can't get you access over it. It's a no fly zone."

Zed shivered. "So, I go by foot."

"Suicide. The entire thing is a maze of buildings built into, over, between, and below an original series of low-income housing complexes. It stretches across most of the city. It would take you days to get to either end."

"Find a pinch point close by. I'll go in a straight line." Zed watched the puddles collect dirty water and imagined a route through a dense cluster of buildings.

"It's not that simple. There are no such things as straight lines in the Wall." Belle's voice cracked and she slipped into a coughing fit.

"I'm not going back to the docks. Point me in the right direction, I'll figure it out."

Belle caught her breath, but her voice was hoarse. "Don't you forget who got you this far, young Zed. You owe me what he has."

"The Captain doesn't have it. Zed does."

Belle was silent, but he could hear her breathing.

"My looking for him is getting his attention, letting you find him, and whatever it is you want."

"You'd better hope you find him before he finds you or he's going to kill you before you know it."

"I have a job to do. I want to get it over with and go home. I didn't come here to chase my tail."

"That's all you'd be doing without my help."

A trickle of rain found its way through the overhang and down Zed's collar. He felt it on his back. The river of bobbing umbrellas surged passed the alley. "It's late," he said.

"You've got that right. Fine. There is a flophouse near you. It's as low class as they come, but I know the owner. You can trust him."

The thought of sleep worked like a magic spell, blanketing Zed in fatigue. He stifled a yawn. "Which way?"

"Into the road, take a left. It's a few blocks, but the entrance is down another side street."

Hitching his shoulders, Zed shook the filthy water from his coat and walked into the stream of pedestrians. Going left meant pushing against it, but he stuck to the side and kept his chin up. His steps became more forced and he longed for a bed, or even a dry bit of floor. Taking a deep breath, he focused on the slog and the throng of people pushing against him.

When he reached the intersection, Belle told him

to take a right. At the end of the block, the street ended in a pile of garbage stacked against the footing of a huge skyscraper.

"It's a dead end," Zed said.

"Yes, but it's also a way in. Look for a switch. A brick to press that doesn't look like the others. I don't remember what side it's on."

Zed went to the closest wall and sighed. Running his hand along the rough bricks, his gaze followed, looking for any aberration in the pattern. When he got to the corner he checked the opposite wall. "Are you sure it's here? I don't see anything."

"It's there somewhere. Keep looking."

Zed backtracked as far as the nearest doorway—a dark stoop a few steps below street level. In the nook, he spotted the faded red mark he'd seen across the city. *Rise.* Shaking his head, he went back to the other wall and searched to the dead end.

"That's it. I've checked it all. Nothing's here."

"It's there. Let me think," Belle said.

Zed heard her mutter to herself, punctuating her thoughts with hums.

"They may have changed their practices. I'll search their dummy site for the information."

The rain picked up and found the cracks around Zed's coat. It soaked his shirt as he jogged to the minimal coverage of the stoop. "I'd appreciate it if you hurried."

Leaning against the door, Zed yawned and folded his arms, shivering intermittently. Eyeing the graffiti, he traced the sharp, blocky letters with his finger and not for the first time, wondered what it meant. "I'm trying."

"What was that?" Belle said.

"Nothing. Just talking to myself. Anything yet?"

"It seems they changed their procedure around a bit. There is a doorway near the dead end, down some stairs—"

The door behind Zed opened and he fell, landing on his back. The interior was dark and several pairs of hands grabbed him, dragging him inside. The door closed as he was pulled away from it, cutting off the dim neon lights reflected off the wet street.

# Ten
## Rise

Zed struggled with the hands that gripped his clothes. His eyes adjusted to the darkness and he could make out three figures carrying him down a narrow hallway. Pulling his feet in, he forced the stranger on the end to move close in order to keep his grip. As soon as his knees were to his chest, Zed kicked out, sending the figure back.

With his feet and legs free, Zed twisted and flailed, giving the other captors as hard a time as possible. One of them responded by letting go with one hand to swing down at Zed. He took the hit and pulled that arm in, like he did with his legs, and wrenched it free. The last stranger struggled to keep pulling Zed down the hall, which gave him the chance to plant his feet and attack.

He'd hunted cornered animals and knew what they could do when trapped. He was no different.

In the near black, he lunged at a dark shape and knocked it to the ground. He swung, landing random blows. The others grabbed at him again and he changed his focus, attacking whichever figure came close.

Someone shouted in the dark. "Stop, stop. Give him space."

Zed breathed heavily. He spun in the narrow corridor, ready to defend himself.

"Hold it. We're not going to hurt you," the voice said.

Zed didn't respond. He faced the direction of the sound, farther down the hallway, and tried to sense behind him.

"Who are you? What are you doing here?"

"I'm looking for a safe house. Somewhere to sleep." Words formed in the darkness, letting Zed know he was being scanned. It reminded him of the implant and the connection with Belle. He tried to reach out to her.

"That won't work here." Zed heard knocking. "You're cut off. Signals can't penetrate the walls."

"Uh, huh." Trying to control the implant, Zed thought of his own scan. A green line ran horizontally down his vision then vertically across. The edges of the corridor appeared in the same green, and the figure was outlined in bright orange. Behind him, Zed could tell there was a door. He assumed it was reinforced, but he couldn't tell from the scan.

"Who told you about this place?"

"An old woman, Belle." Zed glanced behind him. He saw two more people and the door to the street, all outlined in their own glaring colours.

The guy in front of him laughed. "That old bird is still alive?"

"She said there was a," Zed thought of the word, "flophouse around here if you press a brick at the dead end."

"There used to be. It was raided years ago. Who are you?"

Zed sniffed. "I'm nobody. Just passing by."

"What's your name, friend?" The last word was punctuated, and Zed knew the man was serious.

"Zed." The people behind him tensed. One of them took a step back.

"That's not really your name, is it?" The man said.

"It is. I'm from outside the city." The reactions from the people caused a tingle on the back of his neck and Zed prepared to fight again.

"Relax." The orange outline put his hands out. "That's just an unfortunate coincidence. With Belle involved, it's…more peculiar. If you hand over your gun, I think we can offer you a place to get some sleep, but then you have to go."

The others murmured and the man cut them off.

"Hold it." He walked over to Zed and held out his hand. "I'll take that pistol."

Zed reached into his pocket and grabbed the gun. It was solid, heavy and reassuring in his grip. He held it out and the man took it.

"I'm taking a risk, especially with that woman involved. But, we're here to help people, and you look like you can use it. Can I trust you to keep this place quiet, even to Belle?"

Zed nodded.

"All right."

The lights came on, causing the orange and green lines to flash brightly. Instinctively, Zed faded them out.

The man stuck the gun in his waistband and held out his hand again. "I'm Brian. Don't worry about anyone else. As far as you're concerned, I'm the only one here. This group I'm part of is just a hostel—a place for wayward people to find refuge. Like you."

He turned and walked to the door. It opened as he approached. Zed followed and it closed behind, leaving the others in the hallway. Zed looked back.

"Like I said. Don't worry about them. It's just you and me here. Anyone else you see is just in your imagination Got it?" Brian tapped Zed in the chest.

Zed nodded again.

The interior of the building was like Belle's apartment, but larger. The one window Zed saw was covered by a metal plate. The light was harsh. Zed felt it buzz at him. In the back of the room he saw stairs that led up and down.

"Don't worry about that." Brian waved Zed toward the other side of the room with a set of doors on the far wall. "We're going this way."

They went to the door on the right and Brian placed his hand on a pad next to it. The door opened and they went into the room beyond.

It was small, with beds stacked on top of each other along the wall. A chair was crammed into a corner, and a small desk was on the other wall. Another window was covered by a metal plate.

Brian gestured to the beds. "Take your pick."

Taking another look around the room, Zed went to the nearest set and sat on the bottom bunk.

"You're safe here. I'll keep an eye on the door and wake you in the morning. Of course, you could have that implant of Belle's do the same thing." Brian raised an eyebrow.

Zed narrowed his eyes.

"You must not be from around here." Brian smiled. "There are some basic sensors in the room and the door. If I know Belle, you've got something custom. It should be able to connect with them, maybe even override them if you knew how." He folded his arms. "Just, give it a try. Start with setting an alarm and go from there. If you can't do it, forget it. Like I said, I'll be monitoring things, and I'll wake you up."

Brian walked to the doorway. "Get some rest." As he left, the door closed, leaving Zed alone in the room.

Fatigue weighed down on him again. Slipping off his wet coat, Zed hung it on a bedpost. Forcing himself to concentrate, he managed to set an alarm for five hours. He wished he could sleep for longer, but didn't think he had the luxury.

He lay back and tried to use the implant to connect to the sensors in the room, but fell asleep.

# Eleven
# A Coin

A siren screeched and Zed's world vibrated. Launching himself out of the bed, he hit his head on the top bunk. He clamped his hands over his ears and concentrated on his surroundings, remembering where he was. When he realized the sound and motion were in his head, he forced the alarm to turn off and slumped to the floor. The door crashed open. Brian and two others jostled their way in the room.

"What's going on in here?" Brian said. His companions flanked Zed, guns drawn.

"The alarm." He pointed to the spot behind his ear where his implant was.

The guys chuckled and lowered their weapons. Brian sighed and held out his hand to Zed, helping him to his feet.

"Sorry to startle you like that." Zed rubbed the

implant scar.

"You really are new here," Brian said.

Zed sighed. "Yeah. What time is it?"

Brian glanced to the corner of his vision. "Nearly seven in the morning."

"I'd better get moving." Zed grabbed his coat and put it on. "Thank you."

Waving the others out of the room, Brian held out the revolver. "I feel the need to warn you." His brows furrowed. "Belle. We've dealt with her before. She's problematic. When you leave here, she will be back in your head. Just, watch yourself."

Zed nodded and took the gun.

"If you are really going to the Wall, assume everyone is out to get you because they are." Stepping aside, Brian gestured for the door.

"How?"

"Did I know where you were going?" Brian chuckled. "It took some digging, but with a name like yours, I worked it out. For what it's worth, I think you're going in the right direction."

The rest of the building was as empty as the night before, but Zed guessed they had just cleared a path for him. They went through the dark hallway to the door off the alley. The metal slab stood like a barricade against the invasive city outside.

Brian pressed his hand to a box set into the wall. It glowed a faint green light. The door clicked. "One more thing." He held out a coin with deep lines scratched into the surface in the same shape as the symbol. "Take this. It's hard to keep track of what goes on in the Wall, but we've had sympathetic contacts there in the past. If you get into trouble, this may help."

Zed took the coin and slipped it into his pocket. "Thanks."

Brian winked, the door opened, and he pushed Zed out into the alley.

As soon as he was clear of the building, Belle was there.

"Looks like you found them," she said. Her voice was as cold as the wind that whipped around the buildings.

"Accidentally." Zed zipped up his coat and headed for the street.

"And what do you plan to do now?"

Sticking his hands in his pockets, Zed felt the coin. "Cross the Wall."

"Stupid. Stupid and stubborn." Belle grumbled something Zed couldn't hear.

He imagined her cross-legged in front of that big monitor, looking at him from whatever cameras were in the area. "I'll do it on my own."

"You'll die."

Zed rounded the corner and joined the churning crowd on the street. Finding a space, he let the mo-

mentum of the people push him along. The rain had
stopped, but everything was still wet. The wind had
a cold bite to it that in the forest would signal the
end of summer. Zed didn't know what it meant in
the city, if anything.

"I've risked dying since I got to the city," he said.

"Not like this. It may seem trivial to you, but the
Wall is a labyrinth, a trap."

Zed stared ahead, looking for a sign of the Wall
through the muddle of old and new buildings that
towered over everything.

"Your stubbornness is going to get you killed,"
she said.

"Maybe." He looked up at the morning sky,
patches and streaks of shadows crisscrossed in the
air as the sun peered from behind the jumble of
looming buildings. Squinting at the bands of darkness, he looked for the faint outline of a Giant.

"Fine. I can afford to lose an implant if you
throw your life away. I'll tell you where to go, but
that's all you'll get from me. Once you are inside the
Wall, I'll be blocked again." Belle made a wet snort
sound and spat. "First thing, get off that road and
go to Ford Street."

"Where's that?"

"Go east a few blocks. It'll be the biggest street
you've seen so far. It goes a good part of the way
though the city. Get on the Magtram. Then, just keep

going forward until you can see the Wall on the horizon. You'll have to get a few more streets east to get around the dead ends. When you get there, keep going in the same direction to find an open entrance. It'll be the only way in for twenty miles."

"How will I know when I see the Wall?"

Belle laughed. "It'll be the only unbroken slab of stone and concrete on the horizon."

Sniffing, Zed caught the mix of odours produced by the city. He wrinkled his nose and cut across the flow of people, heading for Ford Street.

# TWELVE
# THE LIVING WALL

Ford Street cut through the city like a canyon. The buildings that created the sides seemed to be parted by some divine force, as if the Giants drove them to either side. It was easily as wide as three of the crowded streets Zed had travelled so far. On either side, people milled and flowed like expected, but in the middle there was room for vehicles to freely move. Zed watched them, eyes wide. They zipped past much faster than the train he'd taken into the city. He struggled to make out individual details as they moved. He gave up and found the nearest Mag-tram platform.

At the end of the street, growing as he moved closer, he spotted it. the Wall wasn't as tall as the new buildings that straddled over the old ones, but it was as imposing. It stood steadfast against the current of the street. Even the overhead trains hanging from rails were turned aside by it.

Eventually, Zed could make out the individual structures that made up the Wall. Wide squat buildings made of pale brick or stained concrete, were connected with a mottled mix of materials making a patchwork facade. Structures made of everything from stone to wood extended from the top, more than doubling the original height. From the outside it looked like an impermeable barrier with windows and doors blocked up or barred. Zed huffed as Belle's warnings sunk in.

He got off the tram and took a pedestrian bridge across Ford Street. Heading east, he looked for a road that led to the Wall. He found himself under a building that straddled the side street. A partially destroyed dead end opened to a small overgrown field, the first open space Zed had seen since the docks. It was broken up by strips of crumbling concrete and spotted with piles of rusted metal or stone. Stepping past the dead end, he saw the field stretched along the Wall as far as he could see in either direction. Most major roads ended in a building or were bricked closed. It was as if the city itself came to a dead end.

The lack of people put him on alert. He stiffened as he stepped out of the shadow and strode to the middle of the ribbon of land. Even the noise was muffled. Zed looked to the east and spotted the sun hanging over the Wall. He clung to the city side, he headed towards it, watching for the opening.

Walking on the soft earth made the long trek easier. Zed flexed his toes in his boots and winced as a muscle twitched. He ran his hand through the tall grass and smiled. The solitude and natural environment, even stunted, put him at ease.

Belle cut into the relative silence. "You're too relaxed. Don't let your guard down. If someone in the Wall doesn't like the way you look, they may just pick you off from a window and be done with you."

Zed had forgotten Belle could read his vital signs. He tensed and scanned the barred and blocked windows for any sign of people. Tripping, he looked down and, as if to prove the old woman's point, saw a rotting corpse obscured by the grass.

"Use your head, young Zed. Keep that hunter's instinct sharp."

In the distance, Zed saw a wide sidewalk cutting through the long field. People were gathered at a huge gate built into the Wall and a few folks were coming and going. Taking a deep breath, he walked towards the group.

As he got closer, he noticed some of the people were armed and stood like guards on either side. Zed peered past them and saw the interior of the Wall for the first time. Narrow gaps between buildings were made smaller by makeshift stalls and hovels.

People squeezed passed each other through the tight corridors. Balconies and fire escapes were made into a second level that shook as people traversed it. Above that Zed could see a third walkway before the arch of the gate cut off the view. It was like the city in miniature, more cramped, more full, more dangerous.

A man at the start of the crowded corridor, as old as Belle, but more shabby, beckoned him from a rickety counter made from rotted wood. Zed approached, but was stopped by one of the guards.

The man dressed in dirty clothes accented with solid pieces of debris like crude armour held out the end of his rifle, barring the way. A woman next to him, similarly dressed, stepped forward.

"Where do you think you're going?" she said.

Zed looked down at her, then into the opening. She was smaller than he was, but held herself confidently. "In there."

"Why?"

"To get to the other side."

The man chuckled.

"You think this is funny?" The woman poked Zed in the chest.

Zed furrowed his brow. "No."

She scowled at him. People walked around them, giving them as much room as possible in the narrow opening.

"Why are you stopping me?" Zed asked.

"Because I don't like the way you look. Something is off about you." She spat at his feet.

Zed felt the weight of the gun in his pocket, but he didn't think there was any way the same quick draw trick was going to work for a third time. "I just need to get to the park on the other side of this Wall. I'm not here to cause any trouble."

"I'll be the judge of that!" The woman nearly screamed the words. She walked around Zed, looking him up and down.

The man at the counter waved his arms. "Let him though. He'll just get lost anyway."

"Shut up, Graves," The woman said. She gave Zed another once over and motioned him to go through. "Good luck, funny man."

Zed clenched his teeth. He had to shuffle past the guards who wouldn't move out of his way. He forgot them as soon as he was through the entrance and into the Wall. The single passage he could see from outside was a fraction of the real interior. Alleys and walkways jutted out in all directions, some no wider than the space between the guards. Staircases and ramps lead up and down. Zed turned in a circle, looking for any sign of which way to go.

Graves slipped from behind his counter and took Zed's arm. "This way, come this way."

Zed let himself be pulled to the man's counter.

Sheaves of real paper were piled under scraps of metal. A terminal, much smaller and deeper than the one Belle had, glowed green.

"What brings you to the Wall, traveller? Are you here for the Heart?" Graves took his place behind the counter.

"I'm just passing through."

Graves cackled hoarsely, much like Belle. "No one just passes through the Wall. Everyone comes in for something, and no one comes in without passing Graves' information desk. I can point you in the direction of anything you desire, for a modest fee."

Belle spoke in Zed's ear. "What are you doing wasting time with this bum? He's nothing but trouble. If you insist on getting lost, do it quickly so I can either be done with you or we can move on."

"Can you give me a map to get to the far side of the Wall?" Zed asked both information brokers.

Belle huffed. "I told you, no one has a map. Even if they did, it changes so quickly that it would be hopelessly out of date."

Graves pointed a crooked finger at Zed. "Ah. Maps, maps. That is a challenge. I can point you, give you coordinates even, but maps are another story. What are you looking for? Perhaps I can have it brought to you."

"I told you. I'm trying to get to the far side of the Wall. I have business in the park."

"Business. Business is my business, young traveller. I have the most complete library of information of the Wall complex. No one knows more than Graves, but even I can't get you to the other side. Even if there is any way you can go, it would take you to all places." Graves waved his arms. "It would take you a long time. Even locals know only their own section of the Wall. It is ever growing, ever changing. It defies knowledge about itself."

"So you can't help me." Zed headed away from the counter, back to the entryway.

"Wait, wait. You must wait, young traveller." Graves hobbled after Zed and took his arm again. "Why are you so eager to lose yourself?"

The old man pulled Zed back to his counter, huffing to catch his breath. "You are not from here. Maybe from far away. Perhaps used to a different kind of maze. Don't be quick to throw your life in with this lot. Many never find a way back, let alone to their destination."

"I have to go. If you can't help me, you are wasting my time." Zed pulled his arm back.

"Advice. I will give you advice. One for a fee, and one for free."

Zed rolled his eyes. He glanced at his status floating over the man's head. "Fine. How much."

Graves tipped his head to the side. "A mere pittance of...ten credits."

Zed concentrated and moved ten credits from his unlimited stock to the old man.

Clapping, Graves tapped his feet in a little dance. "Thank you, thank you. Thank you, young traveller. First, I give you advice for free." He leaned in closer. "Do not go down from this level. No matter what! It is death to anyone but those in the gangs. Some from below have never ventured to this height." Looking around, Graves motioned Zed to lean closer. "Now, for the fee. The only way to safely cross is at the highest point. If you can get to the top level, a challenge, no doubt, you will find that crossing is possible."

Zed wrinkled his nose at the smell of the old man's breath. He backed away as soon as Graves finished speaking but the gnarled hands grabbed Zed's jacket.

"The witch is listening, no doubt. No doubt. She is a master of lies who brings abominations to the world. Death is her consort. She will bring you misfortune, no doubt. The abomination holds too much sway within the city. You have no chance to face him here. Go out, go out, drive him from this world to the one you know as your own. Only there can you bring him to a proper end." More quickly than Zed would have guessed, Graves let go of his jacket and grabbed his head. "Do not forget who holds the information here."

# THIRTEEN
# Do Not Enter

Scratching the side of his head where Graves had grabbed him, Zed wondered if the old man had lice or if the itching was imaginary. He'd lost contact with Belle. She told him not to get killed. The warning Graves gave him about Zed stuck in his mind. He didn't remember telling the old man anything about it, but the advice seemed important.

The corridor that ran straight from the entrance narrowed the farther Zed went. It continued to get tighter, but that didn't stop people from cramming more booths in the too small space. the walls were periodically broken up with doors or even more narrow alleys, some formed by the construction of the original buildings, some crudely hewn in odd places. Most of the walls were rough brick Zed scraped against while negotiating the passages along with a near constant stream of people. Some were sitting, or lying in the tight, dark route, which made his progress more difficult.

The corridor cut sharply to the right and ended in a point too small for Zed to get through. He turned around and headed to the nearest alleyway. The passage was tight, but Zed shimmied sideways and sucked in. It twisted and turned, leading to dead ends and more junctions. A few openings headed into buildings, but the corridor rarely widened.

Down one direction there was a hole in the ceiling and Zed could see a shaft of faint natural light. At the bottom was a pile of refuse he stepped over. The alley made a sharp turn and Zed had to feel his way around it. When he was in the joining passage, he saw it ended in a wall a hundred metres farther down. A symbol stood out in the layers of spray-paint. It looked like the mark he'd seen, the one on his coin.

"Shit." Reaching back around the corner, he debated the manoeuvre. He sighed and shimmied forward instead. Near the dead end was a closed door set into the wall. It gave him a bit of breathing room. He slumped his shoulders and relaxed in the tiny bit of extra space

He tried the handle, but it was locked. It gave a bit when he pushed on it, so he braced himself against the wall for support and tried again.

The door cracked and the hinges gave. It opened

backwards and Zed let out a yelp as he fell forward, crashed into a discarded chair, and fell onto the dusty floor.

The room looked abandoned or forgotten. Zed coughed and brushed himself off as he stood. The faint light from the doorway left most of the room in darkness. He willed his implant to compensate. Glowing lines appeared, framing walls. The space was small like the room at the hostel. Old furniture, a sagging couch and a low, lopsided table, were the only things Zed saw, other than the wooden chair half-crushed under the cracked door. Running a finger over the table, Zed cut a deep swath into the layer of dust. He grimaced at the mound he'd collected and slapped his hand on his leg, sending the tiny particles flying.

Along the far wall he saw a closed interior door. It opened easily, swinging inward. Sunlight, like a solid beam, flooded the interior and overwhelmed the implant. Zed shielded his eyes and the low-light mode shut off. The adjoining room was mostly missing. An exterior wall to his left was blown inwards, leaving bricks piled and scattered across the floor. The far wall was completely gone, except for a low, uneven portion about a foot high. Beyond the room was a courtyard shaped like a lopsided rectangle, a few dozen metres across. Zed stepped over remnants of the wall. Tall grass grew around patches of pavement and up through cracks. As far as Zed could tell, the courtyard was completely enclosed. It was peaceful. The constant sound from the city and the incessant din of the Wall were dampened. Zed closed his eyes and took a deep breath. He reached out and let the grass brush across his hand, the murmur almost sounded like rushing water, like the stream that ran through his family's land. He sighed and looked up. The sun was at the edge of the opening, slowly moving behind the buildings to the West. Shadows crept up the walls.

A shape skittered across the shadow-scape, like a person, but too skinny, too many protrusions, oddly proportioned. Zed put his back against the closest wall and drew his pistol. He felt eyes on him and slid across the brick, peering into dark corners. He was trapped, like an animal in a burrow. The way he came in was a maze of corridors so narrow he couldn't turn around in them. If something were hunting him, he would be an easy target.

The wall he stuck to had a hole, smaller than the one he used to get into the enclosed space, but big enough for him to get through. Scanning the scene, he turned his back to whatever was watching him and dove through the opening.

Zed landed on a pile of bricks on the other side and groaned. The room was dark, but his implant compensated. The neon lines imposed on the walls showed a doorway at the far end. Running over to it, Zed saw it was staircase leading down. The outlines provided by the implant stopped before they reached the bottom. With barely any light in the room, he couldn't see far. The words of Graves stuck with him, the warning to never go down in the Wall.

He crept back to the hole, readied himself next to it, counted to three, and looked back into the courtyard.

He caught the shape darting from one shadow to another before he pulled back into the safety of the room. He thought it could have been his target, the other Zed. Maybe. Gritting his teeth he checked his pistol. It was loaded and he had a partial box of bullets rattling around in his pocket. Sooner or later, he'd have to face the creature, but he expected to have set up the trap, not the other way around.

"No time like the present," he muttered to himself.

# Fourteen
# The Beast

Zed leaned against the wall, next to the opening, and searched as much of the courtyard as he could see. The shadows were deepening as the sun moved behind the peaks of the buildings that topped the Wall. Distinguishing the shape of the once-man from the darkness was impossible. Zed willed his implant to outline the scene. Edges of buildings glowed, green, yellow, red, orange, but the shadows in between remained black voids.

Zed could feel his heart beating and his blood rushing in his ears. He focused on his breathing, a technique his uncle taught him while hunting. He changed his grip on the pistol then changed it back, wishing he had his rifle. Shaking the distractions from his mind, Zed counted to three again and jumped across the opening. Flattening himself against the brick, he scanned the other side of the courtyard.

There was no movement. Both the implant and his eyes failed to spot the shape of the other Zed. He'd hunted more animals than he could keep track of, some of them dangerous, liable to attack if provoked. He'd never hunted another person, or whatever Zed was. A nasty feeling churned in his stomach. He shook it away and looked up to the sliver of sky he could see from his cover. He looked for the dim, hazy outline of a Giant in the fading light. Some reassurance he was doing the right thing.

A dart of motion drew his attention back to the ground. "Too late." Gripping the pistol tightly, he squinted, teeth clenched, peering into the darkness. The shadows shifted and he fired. The implant tracked the bullet as it struck a wall. The sound bounced back at him, multiplying as it climbed to the open sky.

Zed pulled away from the opening and cursed to himself. He counted again and steadied his breath. As slowly as he could, he crept back to the hole in the wall, expecting retaliation. Rocking on the balls of his feet, he prepared to jump across the hole again. A flash, much brighter and faster than the outline of the bullet he fired, screamed into the opening and exploded against an interior wall. Zed clenched his eyes tightly and threw his arm up to shield his face. Hot flecks of brick peppered him, scorching his coat and burning his face.

Something struck the wall from the outside, knocking him to the ground. Loose brick covered him. He pushed it aside and saw the hole he'd been leaning next to was twice as big. Zed crawled back, away from the opening. Another dart of movement caught his eye. He dropped to his elbow and fired. The implant tracked the bullet and showed a pulse as it connected with the figure running for cover.

Zed rolled, keeping the shape in the frame of the opening, and fired until the pistol was empty. Several of the shots registered hits, but the figure didn't stop moving. Zed could make out a gangly shape, like a man with things sticking out of him, as it awkwardly juddered away. The bullets didn't slow it down though. It darted into a corner and blended with the shadows.

Getting to his knees, Zed pulled out the box of ammunition and reloaded. "When I shoot you, you're supposed to fall down."

From the corner, more flashes streaked towards him. Zed scrambled to his feet and turned around, stumbling over fallen bricks. He crawled for cover as a piece of the back wall was blown inward. The new hole was dark. Even with the implant, Zed couldn't see what was behind it.

Grimacing, he looked from the new opening, to the stairs, to the quickly crumbling wall he was using for cover. The light from above was dwindling. Shadows grew across the courtyard. Zed took a deep breath and jumped in front of the doorway. He levelled his revolver and scrambled to find the shape of his target. He caught movement and fired but hit a wall. Huffing through his nose, he stood firm. With another perceived scurry, another bullet was gone. Zed chewed on his cheek and waited for the other Zed to retaliate.

Coming towards him, from up high, the shape lunged. Zed fired until his revolver clicked uselessly, but it didn't flinch. He rolled away from the opening as the other Zed landed, but a slash caught him. It cut his leather jacket and left a fine graze across his shoulder. He swung again and struck brick. More of the wall crumbled under the impact, sending Zed farther into the room. Pressing against the back wall, Zed was between the stairs going down and the dark hole. The figure, now close enough to be outlined, twitched and swivelled to face him. The warning from Graves pushed him to the hole.

Zed scrambled through, falling on the other side. Neon lines pulsed at the edge of his vision, but he couldn't make out the room. He heard muffled sounds, like rhythmic droning. Taking a step, he bumped into something solid and realized he was in a closet. He felt for a door, found a knob, and twisted, tumbling to the ground again. He breathed heavily, his heart still pumping hard. The sound, briefly clear, was replaced with murmuring. Light, possibly from the waning sun, shone across the floor in wedges of colour. Zed looked up to see a congregation staring down at him. A stained glass window, like one his father had, but much larger, loomed behind the scene. Zed couldn't tell who they were praying to, but it didn't matter. Getting to his feet, he hurried to the exit, keeping his head low.

The door led back outside to a promenade lined with people and shops. It was wider than the entrance path, but more cluttered. Paths and alleys pockmarked the walls and the makeshift ceiling was higher. Zed spotted a fire escape that was open to the next floor. Pushing over to it, ignoring the beggars and shop-keeps, he saw it went up several levels unimpeded. He stepped over and around the vagrants sitting on it as he climbed. Every floor was a jumble of people, junk, and maze-like corridors. The higher he went, the less crowded it was. Everything was still made of scrap and filled with junk, but the din quieted to a hum. Zed stuck with the fire escape until it came to an end at the original top floor of the building, seven stories up. The building continued, but in a different colour brick with patches of concrete and rock scattered throughout.

Zed peeked through the window at the top of the stairs. It was grimy, but he could see a hallway on the other side. It seemed empty, and at the far end, he could see a stairwell. He tried the window, but it was locked. He bit his lip and scanned the corridor around him. Letting out a puff of breath, he smashed the window with his elbow and cleared away the debris with his leather-clad sleeve.

Someone yelled as Zed crawled into the hallway, spurring him on. He jogged to the stairwell. The steps leading up were made of worn wooden planks that ascended through a jagged hole broken into the ceiling. They groaned as he stepped on them, but held his weight. He continued to go up, making it to the top floor. He found an opening, like a window without a frame, or glass, and looked out over the Wall. He was tired, but other than a few peaks that extended over the exterior façade, he was at the top.

Concentrating, he tried to contact Belle. He heard her hoarse breathing from inside his ear.

"Belle, can you hear me?"

"Yeah. Looks like you haven't gotten yourself killed yet." She gasped in a breath.

"No. He was here. He found me." Zed leaned out of the opening and looked down the way he came.

"Yeah. That was bound to happen. You ran I take it?"

Zed sighed. "Yes. I was unprepared."

Belled chuckled. "He's got your scent now. I can

keep him at bay, but he'll get through my firewalls eventually. He knows what's been tracking him."

"I need to get somewhere where I can be ready for him. Set up a trap." Zed stared at the city that continued beyond the Wall. It was just as impossibly huge as the part he'd already crossed, reaching much higher than where he was. The far side of the Wall was close, though. From the open space, he saw vehicles traveling through the air. He squinted at them, expecting to find a hidden wire or to discover they were an illusion. Several coming from above the skyscrapers turned away before entering the open canyon of the Wall, but one continued on its course.

"You could keep going to the park. It may feel like home to you." Belle laughed again. "It's probably the best chance you'll get. He'd have the weakest connection to his body there."

"Uh, huh." Zed continued to watch the ship as it approached. It was as if it was coming towards him. "There's something—"

"—I see it. It's a corporate ship. Run!"

"What?" Zed had to lean farther out and look up to see the ship as it descended onto the roof of the building he was in.

"Run you idiot! That is something way too big for you to handle! Run!" Belle hacked and wheezed as she yelled.

Zed did as she said. Her tone, her forcefulness,

scared him. He ran to the stairwell, but didn't know where to go. Down was backtracking, and a chance to run into the other Zed before he was ready. Up was whatever threat the ship posed. Grimacing, he went down, skipping steps as he went. The boards shook as he landed, but he ignored the sounds they made. On the floor that he thought connected with the roof of an adjoining building, he jumped off the stairs and sprinted down the hallway. He stopped at the window and saw he was one floor too high. Sounds from the stairwell grew louder. Opening the window, Zed crawled out. He let himself dangle as low as he could and dropped, rolling as he hit the roof.

Zed grunted as he landed, but nothing broke. Continuing across the roof, he jumped the gap to another building and found himself at the outer wall. The roof was pitched slightly and made of tin sheets. They clanged as he walked across them. He went to the edge and saw the floor below with a balcony under the overhang of the roof. Dropping over the side, he swung to the balcony, but slipped. He landed on the railing, pushing out all his breath. He clambered onto the balcony, dropped to the floor, and wheezed.

A man sat on a chair, watching him. Zed put up his hands.

"I'm sorry. I'm not here for you. I'm just, I don't

know. Passing through."

The man yelled at him in a foreign language, the implant translating the foul words he screamed.

Shrinking away, Zed got to his feet and found his way out. The building had a staircase that went right to the ground floor. A well-secured door led outside. He would have never been able to get in from outside, but leaving was no problem. He was at the exit gate, or the entrance from the other side. People wandered in and out in the dusk. Zed stuck his hands in his pockets and joined them. The coin he'd been given was gone, lost somewhere in his escape. He shook his head as he passed the gateway, leaving the Wall with the other Zed in pursuit.

# Fifteen
# The Sheltered Woods

The moon caught him by surprise. It was low over the tree line and looked huge. He had forgotten what it could look like outside the city. The trip from the Wall was nearly the same on the other side. The city simply continued as if the impassable barrier didn't exist, except for the forest. Between an old high-rise and the base of a newer skyscraper, Zed saw the trees. The feeling of open freedom washed over him, but the pressure caused by the implant kept him grounded. He nearly sighed with relief at the greenery.

Belle's voice cracked in his ear. "Don't wet yourself with excitement, now. They're just trees, and he's still after you.

"Any sign of him?" Zed put his hand against the rough bark of a tree. The implant attempted to mark everything in the illusory neon outline, making a wash of glowing colours. Zed concentrated and turned it off, leaving only the moonlight.

"Too much. He's been closing in on me, knocking down my firewalls like cardboard—so take care of it."

"Yeah." Zed bounded into the woods. He kept his head low like his uncle taught.

"And watch out for the weirdoes in there. Though, you'd probably get along with those freaks."

Zed inhaled the air. It was still filled with the rotten smells of the city, but there was a hint of the forest, almost like a memory of his home. He looked up to the huge moon and scanned for the stars he used for hunting and navigating his own woods, but light spilled over the top. Chewing on his lip, he focused on the ground. He searched the trees, looking for places to set up a snare, pit, or deadfall. Thinking of the other Zed made him look over his shoulder. His pistol was full, but he knew that wouldn't stop it. In the back of his head, he had the start of an idea. Something Belle mentioned about the forest and the ramblings of Graves, but he had to worry about the immediate threat. He grabbed at branches as he ran, feeling for the right age, young and pliable enough that he could pull off strips. He collected on the move and wove the strips without thinking, making an approximation of a rope for his traps.

Like everything in the city, the forest was big. There seemed to be no end to it. Zed moved quickly, keeping ahead of his prey-turned-predator. If it weren't for the buildings looming over every horizon, he could have convinced himself he had left the city behind. He stopped in a small roundish clearing to catch his breath. He huffed and thought about home. Shaking his head, he checked how much rough rope he had and cut another branch free. Most of the ground was hard packed. Without a shovel, he wasn't going to be able to dig a pit. A snare was his best bet.

Zed pulled at a branch, a little thicker than he'd like, and heard a snap behind him. In a blur, he let go of the branch and pulled out the revolver as he spun. The implant reacted to his movement. Almost without thinking, it picked between the trees, pointing out warm bodies. There were half a dozen of them—human shapes marked in red and yellow splotches. They hugged the tree-line and would have been tough to spot without help.

Letting his arm drop, Zed cleared his throat. "I can see you there. I'm not any trouble for you and I'll be gone soon."

The figures shuffled together, still out of sight. Zed turned off the assistance from the implant and tried to pick them out in the moonlight. He could see movement, but doubted he would have if he didn't know where to look.

One of them stepped closer. "You don't belong here." His voice was deep and raspy.

"I know." Zed put the gun back in his pocket.

"Something is coming. You brought it," the man said.

"I'm sorry. I needed this place to trap him. I promise I'll leave as soon as it's done."

The man stepped into the clearing. In the faint light Zed could see shabby clothes, a stooped posture. He was thin, but imposing. He spat.

"You monsters are all the same. Not human. Not natural."

Zed furrowed his brows and sneered at the man. Then he thought about the foreign object in his head and sunk. "I'll be gone soon."

"Sooner than you think. It's not far and it's more of a demon than you are." The man stepped back into the trees and Zed heard them all run away.

Belle cackled. "Even they don't like you."

"Yeah."

"They're right, though. He's not far behind you now."

Zed sniffed. "Had to happen sooner or later."

"What are you going to do?"

"Get ready." Zed grabbed at the branch and finished pulling it free. He stripped it and added the strands to his rope.

"Good luck with that," Belle said.

Zed picked a tree and climbed. He strung the rope around a flexible branch and anchored it to the trunk. He dropped the rest of it to the ground and climbed down. He didn't have enough length, so he striped more branches. He fumbled with a strip, shredding it and slicing his finger. He discarded the ruined strip and reminded himself to breath, slow down. Do it right the first time, like his uncle drilled into him.

When he had enough rope, he made the snare and hid it under leaves and debris. The rope was coarse, but it blended in well, and it would hold the thin body of the other Zed.

With his trap set, Zed circled the clearing and looked for a place to hide. He found a bush that looked big enough to cover him when Belle spoke to him again.

She breathed heavily and sounded loud in his head. He stopped and leaned against a tree, winching at the sound.

"Sorry kid. He's gotten past too much of my security. You're on your own now. I can't risk him getting back into my systems."

The connection was cut with a burst of static and a sharp pain behind Zed's left ear. He lost vision in his eye and grabbed the side of his head. He felt warm, slick, liquid, and in the darkness it looked like blood.

His legs gave out from the pain and he dropped to his knees, hard. He rolled onto his side and gagged. He grasped his head and forced it to stay together. He was worried the *pact* was going off, the detonation of the implant Belle threatened him with, leaving his face mangled like hers. The pressure and tearing built behind his ear, twisting through his head. It felt like the implant forcing its way out.

He stifled a scream, bit his tongue, and moaned.

After a blinding, sickening, vague time, the spot behind his ear was split open and the small implant was on the ground. Zed spat blood and felt the puncture in his tongue. He coughed and held the wound behind his ear. It was bleeding, but not enough for him to consider drastic action. He'd been hurt worse, alone, in the forest. He picked up the little implant and held it in front of his right eye. The vision in his left was still fuzzy. He marvelled at how something so tiny had caused him so much pain. It hissed and started to smoke. He dropped it as it flashed and burned from the inside.

Zed crawled to a tree. Pulling himself up, he looked around with a fresh perspective.

The forest he had been enamoured with seemed sickly. The trees were thin and grew crooked in the hard, dead soil. He was disoriented, and couldn't remember which way he came from—the same direction the other Zed was coming quickly. The skyline above the trees all looked the same, and without stars in the sky, he couldn't easily orient himself. He closed his eyes and took a deep breath, scolding himself for not keeping track, for relying on the implant.

His head pounded with his heart, and he felt weak. Crawling back to the bush, he remembered his plan. It was still his best bet, but now he had to deal with the fallout from the loss of the little widget that had been in his head. His limbs were shaky, but he was conscious—in the moment. Probably for the first time since he met Belle.

Thinking of her made him grind his teeth, but the distraction was dangerous. He cleared his head and thought only of the monstrosity coming for him. It had the ability to see him, even hiding in the bush. He cursed and got to his feet. He blushed and realised he was in real danger.

He was prey. Easy prey, so he had to outthink the thing. It was relying on implants, like he had. It could sense things. The trap would be obvious. Zed thought the problem through. He had to find a way to make the other Zed not see the snare. Nodding to himself, he walked into the clearing. He was the target, he had to be the focus, easy to see, but not too obvious. He found a place, right on the edge of the trees. Spotting him would be tough without help, but easy for the original Zed. Once in position, he waited.

Zed kept his ear pointed at the clearing. He knew he couldn't see his target in the dark forest, so he relied on hearing. Every rustle and snap sent a jolt through him, but he crouched, still as the trees around him. Hunting was what he knew. It was how he kept alive. Most of hunting was waiting, and he was good at it.

The sound of crashing grew louder as something approached. Zed didn't think the monstrosity would be so careless, but the other Zed broke into the clearing and headed towards him. It didn't stop, didn't have to search. It moved forward in its erratic motions, a man controlled by strings. Zed counted on having time to lure it to the trap, but it wasn't a man and didn't need to act like one.

Rubbing his bitten tongue on the roof of his mouth, he changed his plan. He stood and walked into the clearing himself. He took out his revolver and held it at his side.

"There you are. I didn't think you'd get the drop on me so easily, but here's as good a place as any."

The figure stopped and its arms flopped like a rag doll. Up close, in the light of the huge moon, it was emaciated and grotesque. Implants jutted out from nearly every place Zed looked. They protruded from the frame of the ghost at odd places, head, eyes, mouth, neck, chest, shoulder, stomach, hip, crotch, knees, feet. It was as much machine as a person and the control was distant and came in jerky motions.

The face behind the implants was hollow. Zed couldn't see its eyes for the machinery and wires ran from them to the back of its head, tangling with others that ran along the body. It was almost a parody of hair.

Zed stepped towards the snare, positioning it between them. "You aren't who you were. Some of you is here, but you're trapped. Belle said you haunted her network. She's terrified of you."

The original Zed didn't move. The two of them stood their ground.

"If you're dead you should leave. Get out of the city, visit the sky. You'll be able to find your way there."

The figure jerked forward and reached out. It moved deliberately and obviously. Zed frowned.

The broken Zed jolted forward and young Zed shot it in the head. The bullet hit an implant and its head jerked back. The impact didn't seem to register with the rest of the body, which kept moving forward.

Zed shot it in the knee.

It dipped, but continued to limp forward.

Zed fired the last few rounds into the body and

backed away. He didn't have to act terrified, his heart pounded. The other Zed kept coming.

Reloading, Zed tensed. He knew the bullets would do little. It didn't slow the thing down at the Wall. He bit his lip and worried the thing would shoot him, or lunge, jumping over the snare. Stepping back again, he drew it closer.

The head snapped up and the other Zed seemed to analyze him with its obscured eyes. It stepped forward, setting off the trap. The rope closed around its leg and jerked up. The creature hung upside-down above the ground and flailed, reaching for Zed.

Zed kept out of its grasp and raised his gun. It mimicked the motion, raising its arm, aiming a blocky protrusion at him. Zed fired first. He unloaded the revolver into the other Zed's head, aiming between the implants. He slipped the few remaining bullets into the chambers and shot again.

It went limp. Its arms dangled above the packed earth.

"Did that kill you?" Zed sniffed. Did nobody try that?" He stuffed the empty gun into his pocket. "If you can hear me, I'm leaving. Going home. If that didn't do it, we can try again out there. I'll be ready, though."

Zed poked the lanky body hanging in front of him and turned away from it. He took a deep breath and found the tracks the other Zed made coming into the clearing—pointing his direction home.

OUT NOW

THE NEON HEART

# Acknowledgements

This book would not be possible without the help and support from a whole bunch of people. Most prominently co-founder of Adventure Worlds Press, Christian Laforet.

Two people who deserve tremendous thanks are my Mum and Dad (mostly for that support stuff) but also for giving this story a much needed critical read. My brothers have always had my back and Jake took the time to read this one over and give me his (supposedly unbiased) opinion.

Fantastic authors Christine Hayton, Michael Drakich, and Edmond Gagnon were generous enough to do some edits for me. Much thanks goes to them (again). Christian also did a full edit for me, but I already thanked him.

Sean Meraw, extremely talented tattoo artist and owner and operator of Radiant Maiden, took the time to design the fantastic cover, and he refused payment. I bought him a coffee, but it isn't nearly enough.

Once again, the folks at Anchor have been amazing, letting me do most of my work right in their way. Thank guys.

**Ben Van Dongen** was born in Windsor Ontario. He likes to think that if he tried harder he could have been an Astronaut, but he is happier writing science fiction anyway. He co-authored the books No Light Tomorrow and All These Crooked Streets, and is one half of the founding team of Adventure Worlds Press. You can read more crazy notions on his website.

**BenVanDongen.com**

Photo by Khoa Nguyen

**ADVENTUREWORLDSPRESS.COM**

More Books by the Author

**The Synthetic Albatross Series**

**The Earth Books**
The Thinking Machine
The Neon Heart
Break/Interrupt

**The Offworld Books**
Broadcast Wasteland

**Anthologies**
No Light Tomorrow
All These Crooked Streets